Merlin, Movies and Lucy Something

John Farman

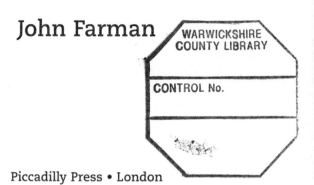
Piccadilly Press • London

To the memory of my dear old gran

First published in Great Britain in 2002
by Piccadilly Press Ltd.,
5 Castle Road, London NW1 8PR

A catalogue record for this book is available from the British Library

ISBN: 1 85340 755 0 (trade paperback)

1 3 5 7 9 10 8 6 4 2

Printed and bound by Bookmarque Ltd.

Cover design by Louise Millar
Design by Mark Mills
Set in Caecilia Roman 10pt

Scene 1

The Kingdom of Joe Derby (my room).
Sunday morning.

ACTION:

'Joe, are you awake? It's your mother.'

And who else would be knocking on my door at this time on a Sunday morning?

I groan loudly, rolling over on to my second-in-command, who farts and licks my face. Words can't describe the sobering effect of his breath. It's my dog, Rover, by the way, who's a long-haired dachshund (in case you were wondering). He's equal best mates with my other best mate, Merlin Labardia.

'What are you doing in there, it's nearly midday. There's someone on the phone – a young lady, I think. Are you going to come down?'

I try to use my voice, but only a sort of wheezy squeak comes out.

'Could you take a number, Mum?'

Let me explain my less than perfect condition. Last night I went to Merlin's mum and dad's eighteenth wedding anniversary party. Sounds boring, eh? WRONG! Boring it certainly was not. So NOT, that I spent most of the evening snogging a fab-looking girl, then managed to force down a few lagers, and ended up sleeping on the floor next to Merlin's 'welcome' skeleton. Luckily for me,

I'd told my parents I was sleeping over. I only managed to crawl home at ten this morning.

Back to the present. I sit up in bed and try to get my head together. It feels like it did after Zoe (my sister)'s wedding – kind of loose and rattly and banging on the sides. It's all beginning to come back to me, just like it does when they have flashbacks in old movies. You know the sort of thing. The screen goes all wavy and the scene changes and everyone looks young. Then it all rolls over me like a tidal wave.

Blimey O'Riley, I've got a girlfriend!

Unless I'm severely mistaken, I've got an actual, living, breathing, not-in-a-magazine, real-life girlfriend. Not only that but, unless I'm very much mistaken, she's got a boyfriend – and that's *me*!

How the hell did that happen? One minute I was sitting on the floor ogling Merlin's older sister Jade (seventeen and gorgeous)'s boobs and wondering if I would have the courage to go all the way for the very first time, and the next I was in the garden with this girl called Lucy something, snogging like a vacuum cleaner (?) . . . and promising deep and eternal love. What was all that about? Then, from what I can remember, her dad came to collect her and I got stuck into Merlin's dad's lager.

The sad, shrivelled organ that is attempting to function as my brain tries even harder. I turn to my canine chum and see if he can shed any light on it, but he gives me an I-wasn't-there-so-how-would-I-know look.

What did she say? Didn't she say she'd always fancied

me like mad and thought I was different from every other boy she knew? That's a bit scary. Let's face it, Rover. I have to live with me every day, so I know what I'm really like. Mind you, she is dead cute – nine-out-of-ten on a good day.

Mum yells up to tell me lunch is ready. I've actually eaten nothing apart from a handful of peanuts round at Merlin's, so I'm quite famished. I crawl down the stairs, completely forgetting that I haven't seen the old folks since yesterday. Trouble looms large!

At seven o'clock last night, before going to the Merlin family party, I dyed my formerly and normally dark-coloured hair practically white with some stuff called 'My Fair Lady', which I was given by Merlin. I must admit the American-looking bird on the front of the box did look much more natural than me, but I bet she didn't do it herself in front of the bathroom mirror (and I bet she was blonde anyway). I wonder if those models do ALL their bodily hair? They don't in *Razzle*!

Dad's sitting with his back to me attacking a dead chicken when I breeze in. When he sees me he looks just like Spencer Tracy did when he first saw his daughter's new black fiancée in *Guess Who's Coming to Dinner?* But it's the expression on Mum's face that says it all. Honestly, if I'd walked in stark naked with my old chap painted like a Red Indian totem pole, she couldn't have looked more shocked.

'Joseph (she always calls me Joseph when she's cross), what in heaven's name have you done to yourself?' It takes me a couple of seconds to catch on, but then I see my reflection in the mirror over the mantelpiece. Oh shit!

Dad looks up and his mouth opens and closes like a fish gasping for air (or is it water?) on a river bank. He stays so long in that position that the chicken, had it been only half-alive, could have been halfway out of Northbridge by the time he came round.

'Have you gone stark staring mad? Go and wash it off immediately,' he splutters, waving the knife around in a most alarming manner.

Unfortunately, Dad appears to be not very well up on the chemical properties of bleach.

'If only I could, Father,' I say with mock self-pity, 'but I fear it might just have to grow out.'

'Who did it? I'll ring their parents and then their necks.'

Blimey, that was almost witty for my dad, I think, quickly trying to work out which joke, if any, might take the heat out of the moment. I decide against saying it was the bleach fairy who'd visited me while asleep, or that it occurred due to the severe shock of learning of my admittance to MENSA and decide to play it straight. After all, that's how George Washington told it when in the same position with *his* dad. (We did it in History last year, in case you're wondering.) And he chopped down his dad's favourite cherry tree, which was much more crucial (actually, we never found out why he chopped down the poxy cherry tree).

'Alas, I cannot tell a lie, Father. It was me. I did it myself.'

'But you look like a bloody queer (his word for gay). What will the neighbours say when they see you?'

'Seeing as Mr Philpot and Mr Williams from number thirty-four actually *are* gay, I shouldn't think that much.'

'Who says they are? Just because they choose to live together doesn't mean . . .'

My dad could watch an over-the-top film like *La Cage Aux Folles* and not notice anything different.

'Oh come on, Derek,' Mum seems at last to be coming to the rescue, 'I think running a florist's called "Just Pansies" and driving a mauve jeep might be a bit of a clue. Honestly, I sometimes wonder which planet you live on.'

'Well, it obviously isn't the same planet as our own pet Martian here (I think he means me). Lord Almighty, to think that a son of mine would do this.'

Mum looks at me again.

'Actually, now I'm getting used to it, I think it looks quite nice.'

Good old Mum, she's bringing in the cavalry to the rescue.

'Have you gone mad, Barbara? The boy looks ridiculous. What will they say at his school? In my day we had to have a short back and sides.'

'Yeah and a stupid school cap and short trousers till

you were practically eighteen. Honest, Dad, loads of people dye their hair these days. You're lucky I don't have a ring through my eyebrow like Spike.'

'At least I'd be able to tie you up outside by it. Really, this is the last straw.'

To be honest, I knew it was going to be a bit tough at first, but my dad can't keep angry about one thing for long and seems to have cornered the market in last straws. There's too many other things to have his knickers in a twist about, like – let me think:

Illegal immigrants trying to wash his windscreen
  at the traffic lights;

Tony Blair;

People getting questions wrong that he knows
  the answer to on 'Who Wants to Be a Millionaire?';

Gardening programmes on TV;

Jamie Oliver (mind you, he's got a point);

The smell of McDonald's as you drive past;

Women drivers;

Modern architecture;

Anyone who doesn't see the point of
  the Royal Family (like me);

  and – most of all . . .

Anyone who seems to be having a good time
  without appearing to work very hard.

* * *

After lunch, I escape to my room and hide. I wait till I hear Mum and Dad go off to visit my gran in the car, then dash down the stairs to the hallway. There really is a number on the pad next to the phone with the name Lucy underneath it.

Blimey, I wasn't imagining it. She still wants to talk to me. I dial the number slowly, wondering what the hell I'm going to say in the cold light of day. Boy, do I hate Sundays – and phones.

'Hello, 8743.' It's a man with a rather posh voice.

'Oh, er, sorry, it must be a wrong number, I wanted to speak to someone called Lucy.'

'Ah. You must be Joe, we've heard all about you. I'm her father. I'll get her.'

'Yes, if you wouldn't mind, thanks.' I hold the phone at arm's length, like a poisonous snake, staring in disbelief. 'We've heard all about you,' he said. Heard all *what* about me? She must have been talki–

. . . I hear the phone being picked up again.

'Hi, Joe, how are you? Did you get home all right? What time did you leave?' It's Lucy.

'Hi, Lucy. Yeah, I'm fine – well, I think I am. I didn't get much sleep after you left.'

'Me neither. When I got to bed, I just couldn't stop thinking about you and what you said. What kept *you* awake, Joe?' She gives a little giggle, but I think I detected a trace of nervousness lurking just behind it.

'No, me and Merlin sat up talking about old films and

stuff. (Our obsession.) The next thing I knew, the bloody birds were twittering outside. The trouble is, Merlin's room's like a crypt – you never quite know whether it's day or night – that's vampires for you.'

'Have you been thinking about me and what we talked about?'

'Of course,' I lie. 'All morning.'

'Isn't it exciting?'

'Yes . . . er . . .what?'

(I'm sorry, but I can't quite get my sad head round all this.)

'That we're going to be going out, silly.'

'Oh, yeah, brilliant. I can't wait to see you again.'

'I wondered what you were doing. Perhaps you'd like to meet me later?'

'Sure, that would be cool, but I really haven't got up properly yet.'

'That's all right. Ring me a bit later. It's a brilliant day, we could go for a walk in the park.'

I put down the phone in a bit of a dream. Hey, I have a date with Lucy, MY NEW GIRLFRIEND! How BAD is that? I punch the air like they do at football matches. Luckily no one's at home, so I do it again. Rover, who's followed me down the stairs, views me very suspiciously. I think he must know I'm up to something that doesn't involve him. I look through the window of the front door and the sunlight stings my nocturnal eyes. This must be what it's like for owls first thing in the morning, when they look out of their holes (or whatever they live in).

At least *owls* don't have to get out of bed.

Scene 2

The Kingdom of Joe Derby.
Saturday, two weeks later.

ACTION:

I'm lying on the bed, wondering what has happened to me since I first started going out with Lucy. I'm feeling a bit like those people you see in the movies who've been in a coma. You know the type of thing. All the family crowded round the bed, shaking their heads at the poor bloke, who's been staring into nothingness for months. Suddenly, their eyes focus and they smile gently, which is the signal for everyone to start blubbing.

It's the same with me. I look round my room and for the first time for ages everything appears as it did before, warts and all. Where's Rover? Where's my best ally? I suddenly realise he hasn't slept in my room for days. Worse still, I haven't even noticed him gone. Ever since that walk in the park with Lucy on that Sunday after the party, I've been like a love-struck zombie – no use to man nor beast (particularly beasts called Rover). My mum and dad thought at first I was sickening for something, because I was so quiet and easy to boss around. They even got me to tidy up my room and take my cups downstairs.

I look up at the bit of wall just beside the bed and survey all the pictures of Lucy that I took with Merlin's digital camera, and then at the stack of her letters and

14

notes that are beginning to spill out from under the pillow. Wow, man, where have I been? – *What* have I been? I start to think back.

The first few days, as I remember, were the worst. I felt my stomach lurch every time I thought about her (which was about all the time). At school I'd hang around just to get a glimpse of her walking about with her mates and I made damn sure we met after school to go part of the way home together. I'd lie in bed, night after night, staring at the ceiling, trying to picture her face exactly and then get frustrated because I couldn't. I remember when I first realised the whole thing had nothing to do with sex. The very opposite in a way – for once I forgot all about it. I just wanted to get into her head. I always had to be sure she felt about me like I felt about her and needed constant reassurance. If she was doing something that didn't involve me, I felt so crap and jealous that I could have trashed whoever or whatever was taking up her time. It was like a ghastly sickness. Then there was food! I usually have the appetite of a fully grown shire-horse, hoovering the fridge whenever Mum's out of the kitchen. Just recently I've been eating like an anorexic supermodel, to the amazement of my mum, who must find the housekeeping money going twice as far.

And *now*? And now, as I reach for my magazines under the mattress, I realise that I'm beginning to feel my old self again (in more ways than one). It's like I'm getting used to the idea that Lucy and me are an item and can feel the pressure coming off.

I open the door and whistle Rover's special whistle. I hear the reassuring scrabbling as my faithful friend builds up speed on the kitchen lino and tears up the stairs as fast as his ridiculous legs will carry him. He bursts through the door and flies on to the bed, licking me like I'm an ice cream melting too fast. I swear he has tears in his eyes.

'There, there, Rover old boy. Sorry I've been neglecting you. Had a lot on my mind, girlwise, you know.'

Rover puts his head on one side like he understands, but I know, from his disgusting performances in the park, that love and romance, in its most subtle and abstract forms, will always be a mystery to him.

But I have to report that things between me and Lucy are beginning to change ever so slightly. For instance, we've had this dumb game we play on the phone every time we're about to finish. She says, 'You hang up first,' and I go, 'No you,' and so it goes on for ages. It's dead weird: I used to find it really funny and cute, but tonight, for the first time, I felt myself becoming slightly pissed off and impatient. When she said, 'You hang up first,' . . . I did!

And another thing: why does she keep going on about me not having a mobile, when she knows I can't afford one?

And another thing: why does she have to tell me what we're doing at the weekend? It's as if I, Joe Derby, no longer really exist as a person in my own right.

And another thing: why does she have this habit of checking her reflection in shop windows every time she passes one?

And another . . .

Look, I'm still into her, of course, but I'm just beginning to suss that the pedestal I'd sort of lifted her on to, might just be beginning to totter. Maybe she's not quite *Lucy Something, Goddess of All Things Perfect*, after all.

I suddenly feel desperately hungry, like I've been on some kind of ghastly hunger strike . . . and then – out of the blue – for the first time in ages – I wonder what my mate Merlin's up to.

Is this a sign?

Lucy Something's house.
Sunday 4.00 p.m.

ACTION:

It's Sunday, and I've been invited over to meet Lucy's parents. I'm dreading it.

I'm just about to leave my place when I realise I'm still wearing my normal slobbing-around-on-weekends clothes. Once a slob always a slob, my dad never fails to point out. I dash upstairs and put on my new black jeans and T-shirt – it is the first time I'm meeting her old folks after all. Just as I'm checking myself over in the mirror, I notice a brand new, never-seen-the-light-of-day-before spot, right on the side of my nose. How attractive is that? The idea of having to talk sensibly in front of her mum and dad with a spot on my nose is enough to make me go back to bed.

Lucy's parents' place, as I might have guessed, turns out to be on the new executive estate on the outskirts of Northbridge. Brand new, but made to look old-fashioned: loads of mock Tudor beams and stuff, with big BMWs for the blokes and little Mercs for their wives. Talk about Smartsville; the sort of houses you'd imagine game-show presenters live in – just an incy-wincy bit poncy. Still, we mustn't be too cynical, must we? Let's face it, Lucy could be my future wife, co-founder of the new

Derby dynasty. Scary or what!

Even so, I'm thinking, as I cycle into the tree-lined estate, any one of these houses would have set her old man back a fair whack.

I find the right number and spot Lucy's dad, or the guy I presume to be Lucy's dad, tearing around the garden on one of those sit-on mower things. All the houses have got those gardens where the lawn runs right round joining the front up with the back like you see in American films like *Father of the Bride*. I must admit, the guy-I-presume-to-be-Lucy's-dad looks much younger than my old man and has the sort of clothes that people wear on those holiday programmes that seem to be on telly all the time.

'Hi there,' cries the guy-I-presume-to-be-Lucy's-dad. 'You must be Joe. I'm Lucy's father. How's it going, man? Welcome to the old shack.'

Old shack? If this is a shack, we Derbys live in a cardboard bloody box. And what's with the *man* bit?

'I think the girls are inside,' he goes on heartily. 'Go on up to the house while I finish this off.'

I think for a minute that Lucy might have a secret sister she hasn't told me about, but then realise that her dad probably means her and her mother. Oh dear, I don't like the way this is going at all. It's all turning into a Mike Leigh movie. Mike Leigh, by the way, is one of my favourite directors. He spends most of the time taking the piss out of the British class system, which is double OK by me. Try *Life Is Sweet* or

Abigail's Party.

As I get near the front door, Lucy and her mother (or *could* it be the mystery sister?) trip out on to the front porch with one of those little dogs called a Shit Sue, or something. It's the kind of dog where you can't tell the front end from the back, except for the bow on its head – God help us if they ever put a bow on its tail. Blimey, I think, if that *is* her mum she's a bit of a babe in her own right – just like her daughter, but sort of *more* – if you know what I mean. I must admit, if that's the way Lucy's heading, it bodes well for the future.

'You must be Joe,' she says in a low, sexy voice. 'I'm Lucy's mother. Call me Julia.'

As she gets closer, I can see the little give-away lines round her eyes – but hey, let's not get too picky.

'We've heard all about you from Lucy. Why don't you come round to the back? We're just about to have tea by the pool.' (By the pool? Blimey, I had a feeling her parents might be a bit posh, but not swimming pool posh.) I feel a bit like a champion dog at Crufts. Next thing I know, Lucy'll be trotting me round the lawn to show off how I move and running her hands all over me to see what condition I'm in. Mind you . . .!

'Hi, Joe!' Lucy runs forward and kisses me full on the mouth, tongues and all. I feel myself going red and try to fight it. That always makes it worse. What is blushing all about? Why does all the blood rush to your head and not your hands and feet? It must be just another of those awful things your body does without being asked – a bit like getting a hard-on when you're not supposed to.

I remember one hot afternoon, last summer, being in our back garden in just my swimming shorts (in just my *tight* swimming shorts), when my horrible cousin Clare (with the brace and big boobs) came round with my Auntie Janet. We were all sitting about, a bit like we're about to do now, when, out of the blue . . . well, you can guess the rest. *And I don't even fancy Clare!*

Behind the house, the Lucy Somethings have a patio by the side of a quite big, blue swimming pool with what look like concrete sea-shell seats round the edge. On the patio there's a table set with tea things.

'Have you lived in Northbridge long, Joe?' Lucy's mum asks.

'All my life, I was born in Northbridge General.'

'Do you like it here?'

Now this is the first trick question. If I say yes, I'll be lying, but if I say no, I could offend her. For all I know she loves the place.

'Yeah, it's OK,' I say diplomatically.

'Oh really? We don't very much, do we, Lucy? We much prefer Brighton, where we were before. There was so much more going on. We had to move because of John's job.'

Now see – that's what telling lies does. By telling a porkie, I've made a right prat of myself. Nobody in their right mind actually likes Northbridge, except maybe my dad and the mayor.

Lucy's eyes meet mine and she gives a little knowing

giggle. Forget all I said about her mum, Lucy looks good enough to eat (except that would be a waste).

Just then her dad bounds up like a frisky puppy who's just fetched a slipper.

'Ah, John, darling, have you met Joe?' says Lucy's mum. 'This is Lucy's father – John.'

'Ah, yes, we're old mates,' he laughs. 'We met round the front. How's it going, Joe?'

I feel like saying it's 'going' about the same as it was five minutes ago, but realise he's only trying to be chummy.

'Er, fine thanks, you've got a really nice garden.'

'Oh, just an old patch of grass to put a couple of chairs on. Have you lived in Northbridge long?' he asks.

Oh no, quiz night again.

'Er, yes,' I glance at Lucy in desperation. 'All my life.'

'And how do you find Northbridge?'

I can't tell the same lie again. Luckily Lucy dives in to rescue me: 'Mummy's already asked Joe that, Daddy. Can we have tea now, I want to show Joe around.'

The next bit of the afternoon goes all right, I suppose. Except that now I can't take my eyes off Lucy *or* her mum, which was not in the grand plan at all. I suppose I've got a bit of a thing about proper grown-up women – I must have caught it from Merlin. Anyway, I might be completely mistaken, but unless I'm going mad, I think I catch a bit of a twinkle in *her* eyes whenever she looks my way. For a second I start thinking about that film *The Graduate*, where Dustin

Hoffman gets off with the mum of the girl he's about to go out with. Stranger things have happened in the twilight world of suburbia.

The trouble with grown-ups is that they, most times, act like a different species to us kids. Sometimes I feel like a hedgehog talking to a fish – no communication at all. Apart from Merlin's mum and dad, that is, who always treat you just like one of them (probably because they've never actually grown up themselves. I hardly know any other adults that I could hold a proper conversation with and that's including my rellies (except my gran). The only thing I hope is that I'm not going to be the same as them at *their* age. My great theory is that if everyone could just be COOL and say the first things that come into their heads, without trying to be polite or correct, we *might* all get along a lot better.

Maybe not!

It's weird, in a funny way I think I actually prefer *my* parents to Lucy's. At least they don't even *try* to be cool. Blimey! I reckon that's the first nice thing I've ever said about them. The trouble is, in this particular situation, with both of Lucy's parents trying so hard to be nice, it makes me feel even more self-conscious than I already am.

Anyway, after about half an hour of this sort of chat, I find myself wishing I could dig a tunnel out of the garden and make a run for it, like in *The Colditz Story*.

Then it happens.

There we are, all sitting round after tea, still making polite conversation, when their little dog (Winkie as it turns out) starts licking my ankle. Without looking, I drop my hand and begin to stroke its head. I haven't noticed, but Lucy's mum, who's sitting next to me, is already stroking the blinking thing's body. Suddenly, I stroke the back of *her* hand, and she gives me a most peculiar look. I whip my hand away and pretend nothing's happened, but just then I feel the little dog, who's quite obviously a boy dog (bow or no bloody bow), becoming over-friendly with my leg. I try to pull it away, but the little bastard's hanging on for grim death – it must be love. Lucy sees what's going on and nearly chokes with laughter. I wait until her mum and dad are looking the other way and then kick my leg violently.

SPLASH ALERT! The next thing I know, the bloody dog's gone over the side, into the old H_2O and is scrabbling for its miniature life. Lucy dives for the pool net thingy they use for clearing leaves, just as the dog's going down for the third time, and scoops it out. It reminds me of a rather skinny rat wearing an all-over droopy, blond wig which, at any other time, would have had me hooting with laughter. The silence that follows is broken by Lucy, thank God, who grabs the opportunity to ask if she can show me her room.

Saved by the babe.

Scene 4

Lucy Something's room.
Sunday 6.00 p.m.

ACTION:

As soon as Lucy and I are out of sight of her parents we start giggling. For me it's half from what's just happened and half from getting away from such an embarrassing situation.

'You sure know how to win over parents, Joe – drowning the family dog.'

'You saw what it was doing. It was trying to rape me.'

'It's only because he likes you. I was getting quite jealous. First it's Mummy chatting you up, then Winkie.'

'That's not what I'd call him,' I say, glancing at the dog which, despite a severe soaking, still seems to fancy me and has followed us in.

As Lucy leads me upstairs, I feel myself getting nervous and excited all at once. It's one thing snogging on a park bench or in Merlin's back garden, but in her parents' house, with them downstairs . . .

Her room, as I might have guessed from what I'd seen of the rest of the house, turns out to be tidy to the point of obsession (or even perversion) – all her clothes hanging up neatly on rails, shoes in line like soldiers on parade, and her larger than reasonable CD collection in well-ordered racks along the wall. In the corner of the large room is a small desk with a laptop and her own phone (pink). By her bed, on a little table, is what looks like a hamster cage with a twitching ball of cotton wool in the corner, which I presume contains Pinky because it's got 'Pinky's Palace,' written on the outside (girls, eh!). On the walls there are a few rather tasteful film posters and, I can hardly believe it, a small piccie of me just as I was looking down her front at the barbecue. She must have got it off her mate Rachel.

It's odd, but I get the feeling, from the Blu-tack marks on the wall, that a load of other pictures have been taken down very recently, which is rather sweet when you come to think about it. Even so, I can't help thinking how totally opposite her room is to mine or Merlin's.

So here I am, alone in her room with her parents' blessing. I must admit, I wasn't really prepared for this. At my house my old folks shift heaven and earth to *prevent* me having anyone in my room – boy, girl, dog or *anything*. Here we're being almost encouraged.

'I think Mummy and Daddy really like you.'

'Er, yes, they're very nice, you're lucky,' I say creepily.

'What are your mother and father like? Do you get on with them?'

'They're nothing like yours for a start.'

I'm about to say something really nasty about my mum and dad, when I realise again that, given the choice, I'd rather have them than Mr and Mrs Upwardly Mobile – Lucy's parents.

'You seem a bit funny today. You did want to see me, didn't you?' Lucy looks a bit disappointed.

'Yes, I really did, honest. Look, I'm sorry, Lucy, but I'm not much good with other people's parents. I'd rather have seen you on your own. This is all a bit sudden.'

'What's a bit sudden, Joe?'

'Well, sort of having a girlfriend. I don't suppose I've really had one before. Not sort of proper. I'm not really sure what I'm supposed to do.'

'Well, you can kiss me for a start. I'm not the least bit proper.'

Blimey, I can't keep up with today. One minute I think I'm about to be thrown out for pet abuse, and the next – oh well!

We lay on the bed snogging for quite a bit and then I notice that her top's becoming mysteriously undone . . . a very strange phenomena indeed, Doctor Watson!

Just as I'm taking my preliminary investigation a little further, the door opens and her mum breezes in holding some clean clothes for Lucy.

'How are you two getting on? Do you need anything?'

Talk about the World Land Speed Record. In 0.000005 of a second flat, I'm about two metres away and still travelling backwards. Lucy simply rolls over and giggles.

'We're fine, Mummy,' says Lucy. 'I was just showing Joe some of my things.'

(You're not kidding, I feel like saying.)

'I ought to go,' I lie, hot with embarrassment. 'Merlin's coming over at six to go through our movie script. Thanks very much for the tea and – er – everything, by the way.'

'Oh you must come round for more,' says Lucy's mum.

Lucy giggles like a schoolgirl (which I suppose she is).

More what? I ask myself.

Back at the Kingdom of Joe Derby.
Sunday 7.30 p.m.

ACTION:

It's later that evening and I *have* to ring Merlin. I wait until I'm pretty sure my mum and dad are stuck into 'The Antiques Roadshow' and then creep down to the phone.

'Hi, Merlin, what you up to?'

'Nothing much, just deciding where to put Quasimodo.'

Let me explain. Merlin's family are not quite what you'd call normal. Not only are they animal lovers, but they're dead-animal lovers too. Whenever one of their pets dies (in this case one of their four cats), they send it away to be stuffed. Merlin's room is like 'Animal Hospital' gone wrong. I'm sure if he had his way, he'd have Rolf Harris stuffed as well (mind you, who wouldn't?). Everywhere you look, you see the whole Labardia family's (including Uncle's and Auntie's) ex-pets – from lizards to snakes, from dogs to budgies – all permanently asleep on shelves or tables. COOL or what? They've even got Jaws, their old goldfish, mounted in one of those special cases, like you sometimes see in posh houses, with the fish's weight written underneath.

'Have you done your Maths homework?' I ask Merlin.

'Are you mad, it's only Sunday? Whatever happened

to Monday mornings? Anyway, what have you been up to today. Didn't you go over to Lucy's place?'

'Sure did. It was like a state visit – I even met her mum and dad – sorry – mummy and daddy.'

Merlin giggled. 'Good Lord! *You'll* be getting married next, if you're not bloody careful. Where do they live?'

'On that new estate just as you leave Northbridge.'

'Not Legoland?'

'Executive Legoland, if you please. They've even got a swimming pool.'

'So what was it like?'

'Oh you know, blue, full of water, with a little diving–'

'No, you spazoid, what was the afternoon like?'

'Weeeeeird,' man! Lucy was brilliant, but it felt as if there was a whole sort of machine all ready and set up to run and I was the last cog needed to make it work.'

'Eh?'

'Well, her mum and dad seemed a bit too keen. They practically encouraged me to go up to Lucy's room.'

'Sounds cool to me,' Merlin butted in. 'How far did you get?'

'You're not going to believe this. Just as it was getting interesting, Lucy's mum walks in carrying Lucy's clean knickers and stuff. She didn't even bat an eyelid.'

'Cool. What'd *she* say?'

'She asked if there was anything we needed.'

'I'd have asked for a condom.'

We cackle like Sid James in the *Carry On* films.

'What's she like – her mum?'

'That's the trouble. She's dead good-looking for an older woman – like a grown-up Lucy, if you know what I mean.'

'Wow, the mind boggles. Hey, we could have a foursome. How old, do you reckon?'

'She has to be mid-thirties, unless she had Lucy when she was twelve or something, but she doesn't really look it. I can't imagine having a mother like that.'

'Blimey, I can,' Merlin chuckles.

'Yeah, but you're a pervert.'

'Mr Pervert to you. What about her dad?'

'Bit of an Action Man. I'm afraid you've cornered the market in cool parents, Merlin.'

I then tell him all about the incident where I nearly drowned their dog and poor Merlin practically wets himself laughing.

'So what about Lucy? Was she all right?'

'Shit, I don't know. She's dead pretty and dead nice and better still, thinks I'm great, but it's a bit weird having a real, proper relationship.'

'Are you crazy?'

'Look, don't get me wrong, I think she's fab and everything, but it's all sort of on a plate. Take it when you want it sort of thing.'

'Aha, the old on-a-plate syndrome. I can't say as I've ever had the pleasure,' murmurs Merlin wistfully. 'Knowing me I'd eat it all straight away and come back for more. Still, at least she's got you over Jade, hasn't she?'

I stay silent, hoping it's true.

'So what are you going to do now, *mon comrade?*' he asks.

'Oh, you know me, probably absolutely sweet FA. I'll just see what happens. Anyway that's enough about soppy girls. We've got to set a date for the shoot.'

Merlin and I, as I said before, are crazy about films, particularly old films, and are going to be in the film business when we leave school – FACT. And we've written a movie which we're going to produce, using Merlin's dad's ace video gear.

'I've worked out a shooting schedule, I reckon it'll take about five days.'

'When's half-term?' I ask. 'We could do it then.'

'About four weeks, I think. My mum and dad are on to help.'

Merlin's mum and dad are the daftest, brilliantest, weirdest, nicest parents in England – no, the world – no, the universe. Tony (his dad) is quite a well-known portrait painter. He makes squillions of dosh which he and Merlin's mum, Jane, spend on their whacky life-style. They must get through the sort of money that would make most ordinary people weep.

'You haven't forgotten my old man's "*do*" on the Friday evening before half term, have you?' Merlin continues.

'Course not. It's up in the West End, isn't it? Can't wait.'

Merlin's dad's having his first really proper

retrospective exhibition of his work at a really snobby gallery in Bond Street. Merlin and I are going up to the even swankier preview to help his sisters, Jade and Sky, opening bottles and tidying up and stuff.

'It doesn't start till seven,' says Merlin. 'So I reckon we should bunk off school at lunchtime and take a look round Soho. It's only games in the afternoon, so they probably won't even notice we've gone.'

'I bet they bloody will,' I reply.

Good old Merlin. If he were a good-looking girl, I wouldn't have to look further than him for my partner. He thinks just like me. I'd never tell him though, he might get the wrong idea. I mean, he *did* dress up as Marlene Dietrich for his party, which was a worry. To tell the truth he looked a lot more attractive than Jack Lemmon or Tony Curtis who dressd as women in the brilliant *Some Like It Hot* (and that's a worry in itself).

Just as I put the phone down it rings again. I'm able to pick it up before my parents even hear it.

'Er . . . hello.'

'Hello, is that Joe?'

'Er, yes, Lucy?'

'Hi, sweet, I just wanted to see if you got home all right.'

'Apart from being attacked by aliens on the corner of Lincoln Avenue, and a group of sharks in my front garden, yeah, thanks.'

'I suppose I really just wanted to talk.'

Blimey, I *nearly* say, I only left an hour or so ago. But hey, maybe this is what you do when you're 'going out'.

'Oh . . . er, yes, sorry I left so suddenly,' I *do* say. 'It was really great being alone with you but when your mum came into the room I – er – well, I suppose I'm just not used to it. I've got armed guards and landmines outside my door.'

'Oh, we don't care about that sort of thing. We've got no secrets. We don't even close the lavatory door.'

'What, not even when you're having a . . . ?'

'No, why should we, we're all the same, aren't we?'

I'm beginning to think I've got the only normal parents in the world. I can't think of anything worse than coming up the stairs and catching my dad or mum on the loo. It's bad enough taking Rover out and having to watch him (and then pick it up). I'm all for modern, but . . .

'Did your mum say anything after I left, about – you know – the bed and all?'

(This is getting tricky.)

'No, why should she?' Lucy replies softly. 'She thought you were very nice and very handsome. She said that if she were my age, she could go for someone like you.' She pauses briefly. I seem unable to say anything.

'When are we going to see each other again?' says Lucy 'I thought tomorrow night.'

I thought: I wouldn't mind a night round Merlin's.

Scene 6

Burger-Babe, Northbridge High Street.
Saturday 8.oo p.m.

ACTION:

Lucy and I have seen each other nearly every night for what seems ages. I must admit, I really like having someone to snog whenever I want, and I think she's one of the best-looking girls I've ever met, let alone kissed. I also think she's kind and sweet and all that. And I like the fact that she thinks I'm the coolest guy in the school, and that all the sixth-form boys turn round and stare at her when I'm with her, muttering snidey things about me. Ha ha!

What I am finding a bit of a pain is thinking up things to talk about. It's dead odd, I couldn't seem to stop when I was chatting her up, but now she's sort of mine, I've run out of steam. It's really funny; Lucy doesn't seem to have a problem with walking along not saying anything, but I find myself humming out loud just to break the silence, which must really piss her off big-time. It would me.

The other thing I'm having deep trouble with is holding hands and stuff in front of my mates. For a start, I think it looks real poncy, and for a second, I'm not completely wild about everyone knowing I belong to someone – even Lucy. This relationship business sure is weird. Suddenly everyone, girls and boys, look at you different, as if you're out of the running, kind of thing.

I got so worried about the thinking-of-things-to-talk-about bit, that on Thursday I asked Merlin if he'd come out for a pizza tonight in a foursome with one of Lucy's friends, a girl called Chloe. To be honest, I don't really know what came over me. I've hardly ever met Chloe, but Lucy says she's very nice – if a bit serious. This does not bode well. Apparently, Chloe has already seen Merlin in Northbridge but, although she thinks he looks a bit of a jerk, says she'll come along because she hasn't been out on many proper dates. This bodes even worse. As for Merlin, the fact he goes for practically anything without a willie is about the worst bode you can bloody imagine.

Merlin's late, of course, and I'm getting nervous in case he's forgotten completely. We've come to 'Burger-Babe', the new American diner-style restaurant on the High Street. There's a really cool fifties juke-box chucking out loud rock and roll and the waitresses or 'Babes' are dressed just like in that fab movie *American Graffiti*. Little hats, stripey shirts, short skirts, bobby socks and, instead of roller skates, white sneakers with bows on. Suddenly, out of the corner of my eye, I spot this apparition in a long, black cloak and blue dreads coming through the door. Everyone in the restaurant turns round, which is just the way Merlin likes it (and just the way I don't!).

'Sorry I'm late, guys. Had a bit of trouble getting my hair right.'

I stand up.

'Merlin, this is Lucy's friend, Chloe. She goes to ballet school in Richmond.'

Chloe's built like a greyhound. A little bit skinny, but dead fit-looking, with a face that will probably be really beautiful one day – not exactly babe-ular but with serious potential.

'Hi, Chloe, I'm Merlin. My sister wanted to be a ballet dancer, but her boobs got too big. I think you have to be really flat-chested to get anywhere, don't you?'

(Merlin, by the way, judges all members of the fair sex by the size of their breasts – seriously.)

I kick Merlin under the table as Chloe goes the deepest shade of pink. Merlin carries on regardless.

'I suppose you don't want to be lugging all that weight around when you're leaping about. Shame really, I reckon it would be a bit more interesting to watch. I personally really li–'

'Yes, thanks a lot to our ballet critic,' I jump in. 'I don't think we desperately need to know what you personally really like at the moment, Merlin.'

'Only making conversation. Hi, Lucy, how's it going with Joey boy? When's the big day? Can I be best man? I think it's terrific, but I'm not too sure about Joe. I think he finds it a bit strange having a girlfriend – don't you, Joe?'

'Er, no, I like it – *really*. Honestly, it's cool – *really*.'

'OK, mate,' says Merlin, 'we believe you. Anyway, I really like to see young people enjoying themselves.

How about you, Chloe – have you got a bloke at the ballet school?'

'No, not really, I don't get time. We have to work dead hard.'

Merlin says, 'Just as well really, they're all poofters anyway, aren't they? – the boys that is.'

She looks miffed. 'Not at all. As a matter of fact they're really strong and masculine, they can pick me up easily.'

'I thought you said you didn't have time for all that.'

'I don't have time for uncouth creeps like you, that's for sure. Sorry, Lucy, I thought he looked weird when I first saw him. I'll see you tomorrow.'

With that Chloe jumps up and storms out of the restaurant.

Stunned silence, then it's my turn.

'Congratulations, Merlin, you've broken your own world record for upsetting someone. You ought to write a bloody book on the subject.'

'What did I say? I thought she looked really nice. Was it something about boobs?'

'Some girls are really sensitive about the size of their breasts – surely you know that?' Lucy says, glowering at Merlin.

'Jeez, I've got a big nose, but I don't run out of restaurants because of it.'

'That's different. Breasts to a girl are a sort of symbol of growing up. It must be awful if you don't have any.'

'So that's why she went into ballet?'

'MERLIN!' I yell, causing all the tables near us to turn round. 'Let it drop for Christ's sake, otherwise there'll just be the two of us.'

'I thought she looked really nice,' he says mournfully. 'I've never met a proper ballet dancer before. Anyway, I went to see Billy Elliot, what more can I do?'

'Let's order some nosh,' I say. 'Can we see a waitress?'

Merlin looks round. 'Jesus, let's get that one.'

I really don't have to look. I can just imagine what she'll be like.

Suddenly, the door to the restaurant opens and Chloe comes striding back to the table.

'I decided that I wasn't going to go hungry just because of Mr Dickhead. Have you ordered yet?'

Merlin looks up sheepishly. 'Look, I'm sorry for what I said. Apparently I've got a bit of a reputation for saying the wrong thing. Can I pay for your dinner as a sort of penance?'

'Unless you can afford a boob job, thanks very much.'

This time Merlin goes bright red and we all fall about laughing. It's the first time I've ever seen him blush – ever.

'C'mon, Merlin,' I say. 'What's it to be – burger or boobs?'

'To be honest,' says the triumphant Chloe, 'I'd rather have the food – I'm starving. We could cook it over your face, Merlin.'

Talk about kicking a man when he's down.

The waitress arrives. I was right, she's a very big Babe indeed. We all look down at the table, trying not to giggle and eventually Chloe speaks up.

'I think Merlin ought to order first.'

Poor Merlin finds it difficult to look up. The waitress's chest is exactly on his eye level. She looks at him as if he's just come from another planet.

'Is there something wrong?'

'Er, no. I'd like the – um – Big-Babe Double Whopper please.'

I just cannot believe he chose that.

Have you ever tried to *not* laugh so much that you think your head's going to explode? I turn away coughing and spluttering and Lucy, who just can't handle it at all, rushes off to the naffley named Babes'. Chloe, amazingly, remains totally calm and collected and speaks defiantly.

'I'll have the Veggie Babe with no bun and a salad, please. I'm trying to watch my figure.'

Wow! This girl won't give in. She's determined to make poor Merlin squirm.

Having said that, as the meal goes on, they begin to get on rather well. Every time he tries to be flash or clever, Chloe comes back with a line that flattens him completely. It's extraordinary. Eventually he finds it really funny, to such a point that in the end they're chatting away, ten to the dozen, about ballet dancing and theatre and all sorts. I'm left with Lucy again.

'I could have bet you a million quid that wouldn't

have happened,' I whisper.

'They're actually good for each other. He needs someone to calm him down and she needs someone to bring her out . . .'

'Did you think this might happen?'

'I knew Chloe doesn't take any crap, and I suppose I knew that underneath it all Merlin's really insecure. Maybe I ought to do this match-making for a living.'

'Do you think you made the right decision with me?'

'I'm not sure. You're still under probation. I fancy you like mad, but sometimes I don't know where your head is.'

That makes two of us, darlin'.

Scene 7

My house.
Sunday, two weeks later, 3.00 p.m.

ACTION:

That's done it. Now Merlin's in love. Completely infatuated in fact. He hasn't spoken about anything else apart from Chloe ever since that night out and it's beginning to get on my nerves. She apparently remains as cool as a cucumber and won't even let him snog her.

So what in the name of real silly buggers is the matter with me? One minute I'm all excited because I've got a proper girlfriend, and then I start feeling trapped. It's so weird. It seems to me that Lucy Something has more or less decided that I'm the *one* and nothing short of me turning gay or becoming a monk (or a gay monk) is going to change things. The strange thing is, that when I'm with her, I think she's dead sexy and all that, but when I'm on my own all the doubts come in. I just can't help it. I know I'm a pessimist, but I keep getting visions of our Zoe's wedding reception and that horrid queue where all the parents and the bride and groom have to shake hands with everyone as they come in. Just imagine having to stand next to Lucy's parents – John and Julia Upwardly Mobile.

Since going over to Lucy's house that Sunday, I must have seen her about a thousand times and spoken to her about a million. Look, I do really think she's nice –

honest, but I feel like I'm being swamped. Girls are dead odd. They pretend to be all sort of interested in what you're doing but are they really?

I suppose I could admit that I'm not really interested in what Lucy does either, but seeing as she doesn't really seem to do anything apart from worry about me and what she looks like, it's not my fault. Meow!!

Now she wants to meet *my* parents. I've tried everything to get out of it, but, unknown to me, she's become really pally with them on the phone. She talks with whoever answers the damn thing, whenever she rings to speak to me – which is all the bloody time! I don't *really* mind, but it just seems like she's trying a bit too hard.

Now, out of the blue, my mum's gone and invited her over to our house (the first time she's ever done such a daft thing), and she's about to turn up.

'Joe, darling,' Mum says, 'go and smarten yourself up. You don't want Lucy to see you in those awful clothes, do you? She'll be here in a minute.'

I can't believe it: Mum and Dad have actually changed. Mum's in one of those ghastly flowery dresses from the ads she cuts out from the back of the *Sunday Express*, and Dad, almost unbelievably, is wearing his navy blue blazer and golf club tie (and trousers too, thank God).

'Blimey, you two, she's only an ordinary girl, not the blinking Queen Mother,' I say despairingly.

Oh hell, I'm dreading this.

Before I get a chance to escape, our naff door chimes ring. She's early. Oh no, here we go. This is going to be mega pants.

Lucy, as usual, looks really gorge in a very short black skirt, whiter-than-white T-shirt, white-than-white plimsolls and a shiny blue jacket. It's incredible, I've hardly ever seen her in the same gear twice (and she's hardly seen me in anything apart from what I'm wearing now).

Dad can't believe his eyes. They practically roll out of their sockets, down his body, across the floor and up her legs. I don't know what sort of birds he thinks I knock around with, but he's obviously not expecting anything as lush as Lucy. He looks back at me as if he simply can't work it out. He then pulls his hand across the remains of his hair in an effort to smarten it up.

Mum gushes forth.

'Lucy, darling, come on in, we've heard such a lot about you.' (*No, they haven't!*)

'Let me take your jacket.'

'Thank you, what a lovely house you have,' Lucy lies, handing Mum her jacket and walking over to kiss me.

Poor Dad doesn't know where to look. One second he's struggling to get over having a young pretty girl in his own front room and the next he's having to cope with the shocking sight of her tongue halfway down my throat. It's just like some exotic butterfly has somehow blown in through the window and settled on the dog (i.e. me!). The real dog (Rover), by the way, takes one look at his commanding officer being passively assaulted by a woman and slinks upstairs to our room in disgust. If he had a bag, he'd pack it.

Oh no, Mum's off again.

'Let me apologise, for our son's appearance. We're always on at him to smarten up. He looks so nice in proper clothes. Joseph, darling, you really should make more of an effort.'

Lucy gives me a rather disapproving glance and says, 'Oh I expect it's just a phase. Lots of boys go through a period like that.'

Hang on a cotton-pickin', minute, you're not supposed to agree with them. I really don't like the way this is going at all.

'I think he hangs around with that Merlin lad too much,' says Dad. 'He's a weirdo if ever I saw one.'

'Oh he's all right, Mr Derby. Just a bit childish,' Lucy replies.

HOLD IT, that's my best friend you're talking about.

'I hope you'll be able to lick our Joe into shape, though,' Mum says with a laugh.

Lucy giggles and gives me a naughty little look.

Now Dad can't believe his ears – or his eyes.

The conversation continues as if I'm not really there. Every dig they have at me, Lucy agrees with. In her effort to please them, she's scoring more and more brownie points for herself . . . AND OFF ME – for God's sake!

After about an hour, they're practically making the flipping wedding arrangements. My dad's been in and out of his shed showing her the stupid things he's made, while Mum's been having sickly all-girls-together chats about make-up and stuff. As for me, I could have taken all my clothes off, disembowelled myself and swung upside down from the ceiling for all they'd have noticed.

It's no good – as Popeye always said to Olive Oyl – 'I can't stands no more'.

'Can I take Lucy up to show her my room?'

Dad pipes up true to form.

'Are you mad? Lucy doesn't want to go in there – she'll never be seen again. I'm sure there are viruses growing in there that there's no known cure for.'

'I'm sorry, Lucy,' says Mum, 'but our Joseph is really one of the messiest boys we've ever known. We really don't know where he gets it from. I'm continually going on at him, but does he listen?'

'I'm sure I'll be able to do something about that, Mrs Derby,' says Lucy, glancing at me in a head-teachery sort of way. 'I'm sure his room's not that bad,' she continues almost condescendingly. 'Anyway it's always interesting to see how someone else lives.'

As it happens I *had* tried to do something with my room before Lucy arrived. The trouble is, it's a bit like trying to clear up after a five-day rock festival – you don't know where to start. Still, I kicked all my old socks and pants under the bed, hid my girlie magazines, stacked up all the teacups and tried to make my bed look less like a dog basket. Then I got bored and, to make a point, Rover, looking well pissed off, was straight back on it making another hairy nest for himself.

Lucy looks round my room and recoils as if she'd been parachuted into a sewage farm. I must admit she does sort of stand out like a pillar of cleanliness.

'Well, your parents weren't exaggerating, were they?' she says when she gets her breath back.

'I think you get on better with them than I do. Blimey, I felt like I was in front of a firing squad.'

'Oh, I'm always like that with parents. It makes things so much easier.'

'For you maybe. All I'm going to get from now on is how much I don't deserve to have a girlfriend like you.'

'Maybe you don't,' says Lucy, with an expression that makes me wonder if there is more to it than meets the eye.

The next hour or so is pretty groovy. We roll around on the bed, kissing each other in just about every way possible until, towards the end, I find myself running out of ideas. Just when I'm supposed to be in the height of passion I begin to wonder what my mate Merlin's up to.

Now there's a worry!

Scene 8

Sunnydale Sheltered Home for Senior Citizens.
Sunday 12.30 p.m.

ACTION:

I've now been what they call 'going steady' with Lucy for six weeks or so and, boy, I am not a happy bunny. If anything, having a girlfriend like Lucy makes me feel even less together than I did before. I suppose it's because I feel so completely unready – almost like I offered myself under false pretences. Still, it really isn't her fault. Mum always says that girls are much more grown-up than boys and if being ready to handle a steady full-on relationship has anything to do with it, I'd be the first to agree.

It's Sunday, and I've just cycled over to see my dear old gran in her sheltered flat in Woodley Green, a few miles from Northbridge. She's the only person in my family capable of convincing me that I wasn't sold to my parents by wandering gypsies (or worse). She's also the only one of them who can really make me laugh.

If my gran hadn't had a bout of chronic arthritis at the time of Zoe's wedding, it wouldn't have been nearly so painful for me either (well, painful until Jade Labardia snogged me, that is). My sister Zoe recently married the ghastly Graham Bunt, and, just as the whole day was turning into a disaster, Merlin's gorge sister, Jade, jumped on me on the fire escape and saved

48

the day – well my day, anyway. Actually, if my gran *had* been there, the whole day might have been a bit of a laugh.

My gran's just as naughty as I am, you see, and whenever we're in polite company my old folks do their best to keep us apart. When I think of my boring, pompous great-uncle Harry, her brother, who's only a bit older than her, it's difficult to believe they're even from the same species, let alone family.

Granny Derby comes from my dad's side and is a real live cockney, brought up in the East End of London. Her husband Joe, my granddad, who'd been a fireman all his working life, died three years ago and, since then, I've tried to get over to see her every couple of weeks. I know she's lonely, but it's mostly because she feels, like me, that most people are a bit of a waste of space.

The best thing about my gran is that she's reached an age where she doesn't really give a damn what anyone thinks of her. It's as if she and I are almost the same in a way, but at either ends of our lives, sort of thing. I wonder if that happens a lot? If she feels like swearing, she'll swear better than anyone and if she fancies a ciggy or a drink – at any time in the day or night – she has one. The more people go on about her health, the more she does it, saying that at her age she reckons she's earned the right to do exactly as she bloody well pleases. Three cheers! I say. Best of all, unlike most people, she really likes my best mate, Merlin, seeing way beyond his rather odd appearance.

As for Merlin, *he* reckons she more than makes up for the rest of my mega-boring family.

I push her bell and wait. After a while I hear her hobbling painfully to the front door, grumbling loudly about being disturbed.

'Bloody Jehovah's Witnesses! Why can't you leave me alone? Just because it's Sunday.'

The door opens cautiously.

'Hi, Gran, how you doing?'

She stares hard as her old eyes focus, then chuckles like a kid when she recognises me.

'Joe, my darling boy, how lovely to see you. I thought you was the God people. You really shouldn't have come all this way on such a day. It's cold enough to freeze your dangly bits. Come on in. How are you? I like your hair. (See!) How's Mum and how's that silly dad of yours?'

'We're all fine thanks, Gran. Dad's still silly. How are you . . . really?'

'Oh, I struggle along. I've decided not to run that London Marathon thingamejig next year, though. I thought I'd give the others a chance. Come in and have a cuppa – I made one of your favourite cakes yesterday. I must have had one of those prelimitions you was coming.' (She always gets long words wrong.)

I really love her little flat. She's managed to cram in all the good bits from her old house. I look round happily. It's a bit like visiting a sort of museum of our family. There's a picture of my late great-uncle Jim (who was also all right) sitting on top of a camel in a silly hat (that's Jim, not the camel) during the war in Egypt; one of my dad from the late seventies, looking really embarrassing with long hair and the most awful flares; a couple of my sister, Zoe, before she turned into a monster; and a big one of me as a toddler appearing as if I was about to be shagged by Chappie, our old labrador (which *could* have accounted for everything). Anyway, who in their right mind calls a dog Chappie?

I continue looking round as Gran makes the tea. On the modern mantelpiece are all the old ornaments I used to play with as a little kid – nothing worth more than a few quid, but priceless to her . . . and to me, come to that. There's the model of the Eiffel Tower to commemorate the liberation of France from the Germans; a little brass replica of a Spitfire made out of a World War Two shell-casing, made by Great-Uncle Jim in hospital after having his leg off; a money box in the shape of a black boy's head and shoulders (very non PC these days); two thirties chromium-plated nude ladies holding feathers over their heads which I thought were ever so rude when I was little, and loads more.

'So, Joe, how's it going?' she asks, once she's put the tea and my favourite cherry cake on the little table next to me. 'We haven't had a chance to have one of our chats since the wedding. Was it terrible? I'm so sorry to have missed all the fun. It was the old arthritis again. I couldn't bloody move.'

I tell her all about the reception: Mr Spotty, the best

man's speech; the first Mrs Bunt running off crying into the lavs; about awful Great-Uncle Harry and the near punch-up at the end.

Poor Gran is almost crying with laughter by the time I've finished, and dabbing her eyes with one of her little hankies which always seem to smell of peppermints.

'Gor blimey, what a carry on. No one mentioned all those goings on. I just got the boring version,' she says as soon as she gets her breath. 'Did you see Hilda there?'

'Yes, she was on my table.'

'Oh you poor lamb, you must have been near starved. Did she eat the bloody lot? Here, have another piece of cake. You look like you need building up.'

We laughed and laughed for the rest of the afternoon. Just as I was thinking about going, I tell her all about MY BIG PROBLEM.

'Well, Joe,' she says after a while, 'here's the advice of a very old, but not-very-wise woman. In my opinion we're all a long time grown-up – far too long in my case. You've got bloody years to do the *right* things – settling down and all that. Play the field is what I say. Don't be horrible to them – that's not nice, but don't let them trap you either. There's a lot of girls out there that think about nothing except getting a man. It sounds like your . . . what's her name? . . .'

'Lucy.'

'It sounds like your Lucy might be a bit like that. Now as for this Jade girl you mentioned, I rather like the

52

sound of her. She sounds as if she's playing the man's game – taking what she wants when she wants it. If I hadn't met your granddad when I did, I reckon I might just have done the same for a bit, and believe you me, times were different when I was your age. You just get on with enjoying yourself. If you feel like you want a proper girlfriend, have one, but if you feel you don't, then you'd better tell her.'

Thanks, Gran.

Scene 9

Soho, Central London.
Friday 3.00 p.m.

ACTION:

It's the day of Merlin's dad Tony's private view and Merlin and I have bunked off games and are about to take the tube up to the West End to have a snoop around Soho before showing up at the gallery. Luckily it's half-term next week, so, with a bit of luck, they'll have forgotten about it by the time we go back.

It's so good to be getting away from Northbridge – the whole Lucy thing is becoming more of a pain than a pleasure. But if I'm having a hard time, Merlin's having it worse. He just can't seem to stop going on about Chloe, the ballet dancer.

As we're sitting on the platform, waiting for the train, he confesses all.

'Joe, I know you're not going to believe this, but I think I'm really in love, like properly. I've never felt like this before and it really hurts.'

'Does she feel the same way about you?'

'You're joking! OK, she thinks I'm funny and clever and all that, but not what you'd call going-out-with material. What have I got to do to convince her I'm not just a shallow bloke obsessed with the size of girls' boobs?'

'Lie through your teeth. Let's face it, Merlin, you are

just a shallow bloke obsessed with the size of girls' breasts.'

'That's so crap! If that was the case, I wouldn't fancy *her*, would I?'

'Good point, but you did make a bloody awful start. Anyway, when did you see her last?'

'Last week. She's gone off to Paris to study mime – it's part of her course, apparently. I'm missing her so much you wouldn't believe. You never told me it felt like this.'

'Come on, Merlin, it's me you're talking to. I bet it's because you can't quite crack it. I reckon if she came on to you big-time you'd be off like a frightened rabbit.'

'It isn't like that, honest. I really, really like her.'

Oddly enough, I believe him.

The train comes and we eventually end up at Leicester Square. Merlin, as always, looks fairly weird in a long, black, nearly-to-the-ground linen coat, pointed boots and hair still in dreads and still dyed a sort of weird electric-blue colour. I reckon he might be wearing a bit of make-up round the eyes but, after the Marlene Dietrich episode, I hardly dare ask.

He doesn't, of course, get quite the number of stares he does in Northbridge. Let's face it, there are people on the street in Soho that make him look almost normal. As for me, I've long worked out that I'm the sort of person that would much rather have a *friend* who's a freak than be one myself, well happy to bask in his reflected weirdness. I'm wearing the nearly black suit, shades and – of course, my fairly new, spiky blond hair. Even so, I reckon we both look pretty cool for a couple of hicks from suburbia and that's what it's all about if you ask me.

I remember once seeing Cliff Richard's first movie – *Expresso Bongo* – filmed all around Soho in the fifties and am amazed how little it's actually changed. I'm also amazed he ever became a star.

I suppose the first thing I notice are the girls – they're far better looking. Practically any one of these smart, black-suited, long-legged, mobile-phoney, West-End chicks would stop traffic in Northbridge. They seem to hover around the bars and coffee shops in droves, suddenly rushing off as if their lives depended on it, to meet their clone sisters (to talk the same sort of bollocks, no doubt). They're like black humming birds in a way, darting between flowers taking a little bit of nectar from each. What the hell am I talking about?

Merlin makes a beeline for a shop called 'She-Male' which sells all kinds of sexual aids and fetish gear. It has a sign saying 'Eighteen Only' on the door, but the girl (I think) by the counter doesn't seem to mind us looking round. To be honest, I feel a bit out of my depth. Half the stuff on the shelves I've got no idea what you're supposed to do with (or even less where to put them). I can't help wondering what Lucy would make of it all. Merlin's in his element, however, trying on leather masks with zips across the eyes and mouth and handcuffing himself to the shop dummy – a girl (again presumably) – with spikes sticking out of her rubber-clad boobs, straps around just about everything that can be strapped and stiletto-heeled, thigh-length, lace-up, shiny black boots. She's carrying a whip in one hand and is clasping a very realistic looking snake by the neck in the other. (Do snakes have necks, or are they all neck and no body?) Just the sort of young lady you'd invite home to meet your parents – not that Merlin's mum and dad would probably bat an eyelid.

Time's moving on, so Merlin suggests we try getting an early drink in one of the pubs in Old Compton Street. I haven't had much luck in pubs so far – I'm always asked for an ID, but Merlin, with his standard-issue half-Italian, half-five-o'clock shadow, can sometimes get away with it. Just as we're deciding who should go to the bar, I get a tap on the shoulder.

'Hello, my name's Douggie. My friend and I noticed you as you came in. Are you looking for anyone in particular?'

Douggie looks about twenty with the same colour hair as mine and a black T-shirt, with the word BITCH emblazoned across the front in sequins, short enough to reveal a ring through his belly button. His mate is in head-to-foot, skin-tight, split-to-the-waist denim, with snakeskin, western boots and a wide, leather belt with a brass buckle saying STUD. I look around and realise that there's not a single girl in the place.

Jeeeeesus! I don't believe it; we've walked into a men-only pub. I feel like a very straight fly in a very gay web. This really is the last time I follow Merlin anywhere.

'Would you like a drink?' asks Douggie.

Merlin, who's just sussed what's going on, butts in and says, 'Yeah, er – thanks, two halves of lager, please.'

Douggie's friend strolls over while he's making his way to the bar.

'Hi, I'm Rik . . . with a k. I don't think we've seen you in these parts, have we?' His rather high, nasal voice doesn't really go with his fresh-from-the-trail cowboy outfit. He sounds a bit like John Wayne with a cold and too-tight pants.

Merlin hesitates for a second and then speaks for both of us.

'We've been abroad for a long time – America actually.'

'What were you up to, were you at college?'

'No, we've just flown in from LA. We've been working out there.'

Rik-with-a-k looks taken aback.

'You poor darlings, you look too young to be working anywhere. What were you doing?'

At this point I'm fully prepared to make a run for it – sod the drink! Merlin on the other hand, seems to be almost enjoying it.

'Oh, we're in the middle of making a movie. We've got to go back next week.'

Rik-with-a-k looks at us first in awe, and then disbelief.

'Well, heavens above! So what are your names? Will

I have heard of you?'

I give Merlin my best let's-get-out-of-here look.

'I'm Merlin Labardia and this is Joe Derby. You might have done, but I doubt it. Joe's done mostly telly and commercials and I was in a couple of low budget movies earlier this year. I think they showed them at the British Film Institute a few weeks back.'

Douggie comes back with the drinks.

'These two young lovelies are famous, Douggie,' he says with a slightly sarcastic tone and then puts his gun-slinging hand on my shoulder. 'They've just come back from LA.'

I freeze like a marble statue and tug Merlin's sleeve.

'Really, how come?' Douggie asks.

Merlin is now in full flow and is even adding a slightly camp edge to his voice.

'Joe's father's in the film business and last year the producers of a movie he was working on were casting for two guys about our age, so he suggested us.'

Douggie then turns to me.

'How absolutely fascinating. What's it about, Joe?'

I glance desperately at Merlin, but he appears not to notice, and continues, 'Oh, it's about two young English kids on their summer holidays in the States with one of their uncles. While he's away on business, they decide they're going to murder the president of McDonald's. They're animal activists you see – and vegans as well.'

I stare at Merlin in complete and absolute awe. Where the hell does he get all this junk from?

Rik-with-a-k turns to me. I can tell he's beginning to wonder if we might actually be on the level.

'How fascinating, we've never met filmstars before. Tell you what, we're going to a new club in Greek Street later – the 'Silver Thong'. Maybe you two would like to come with us?'

'Sorry, we'd love to,' I reply, 'but we have to go to a private view in Bond Street.'

'Reeeeally! How simply divine. Who's showing?' Rik-with-a-k looks genuinely impressed.

'Oh, a guy called Tony Labardia,' Merlin says. 'Have you heard of him?'

'Heard of him? Are you kidding? We simply adore him, don't we Douggie?'

'Is he the one that did the portrait of Julian Clary?' Douggie asks.

'Yeah, it was in the *Sunday Times* last week. It was too scrumptious for words,' says Rik-with-a-k.

'He's actually my father,' continues Merlin proudly. He's now on a roll, completely unfazed by their attention. They're just like putty in his hands.

I notice that a group of curious men have gathered round us, which prompts Rik-with-a-k to put his arm round Merlin's shoulder possessively.

'Well, what a lucky man to have such a talent *and* such a sexy son.'

Suddenly Merlin realises just what he's got us into and looks nothing short of petrified. He looks completely out of his depth and glances across to me to get him out of it. Desperately grabbing his arm, I tell the guys we're late and frog-march him out of the pub still holding his drink.

When we're in the busy, rush-hour street, we both look at each other as if we've been rescued from a lion's cage and then fall about, clutching at lamp-posts and laughing till we almost collapse.

'I didn't think much of yours,' Merlin splutters, giggling almost maniacally, the colour returning to his cheeks. 'I prefer the Lone Ranger look.'

'Don't you ever do that to me again, you muppet. You were as scared as I was and don't deny it. You could have got us into SERIOUS trouble in there, especially if they'd sussed you were taking the piss.'

Close Encounter of the Third Kind, or what!

Scene 10

The DeBoulay Gallery, Bond Street.
Friday 7.15 p.m.

ACTION:

If anyone ever tells you there's no money left in this country, invite them for a stroll down Bond Street, London, on a Friday evening. I've never been here before and can hardly believe what I'm seeing. Men and women from practically every part of the world, who look as if they'd have a fit if they ever had to do a proper day's work, or even cook their own dinner. It's the women that get me most. Talk about refugees from Planet Dosh in the Galaxy of Plenty; everything about them seems unreal. Hair so smooth, shiny and stiff that it looks as if they put it on the bedside table at night; more make-up than a heavy-handed pantomime dame; clothes that look as if they'd cost more than my dad earns a year and shoes that probably have never had to walk further than from a taxi to a shop or restaurant. And they all look exactly the same (the shoes *and* the women), all united by the fact that nobody in their right mind would dream of even talking to them (let alone anything else) without a diamond-encrusted, platinum credit card.

Two rather smart ex-rugger buggers in penguin suits are on the door of the gallery and look at us a bit like they would if a pigeon had just crapped on their lapels.

Merlin, bless him, waves our invites under their six-foot-high noses with a cocky flourish and in we go. I must admit, it's the first time I've ever been to an art gallery, let alone a private view, and I don't know quite what I'm supposed to do or be. The last art gallery I saw was in that dead funny old film, *The Rebel,* with comedian Tony Hancock, all about a bloke who goes to Paris to become an artist.

The first person I recognise, across the large room, is Jane Labardia, Merlin's mum, looking as whacky as ever. For some reason best known to herself, she has chosen the sort of dress that that woman in *The Addams Family* wore – long and black, tassels everywhere, tight as a wet-suit, ludicrously low-cut and dragging behind her on the floor. Her hair is in plaits – one silver and one gold – and she appears to be wearing the most astonishing sea-green contact lenses.

I catch some conversation to my right. A rather limp-wristed man who I reckon must be the gallery owner is talking to, or rather *at*, a rich-looking old bird who looks like she died three weeks ago.

'Really, Mrs Goldstein, you can't go wrong with a Labardia. He is the quintessence of the post-modern school of English portraiture, laced with the piquancy and panache of Venetian Baroque. His paintings live and breathe the fiery passion of the Umbrian hills from whence he comes.'

From whence he comes? What tosh! I feel like jumping in and reminding him from whence he really

63

comes. The real Tony Labardia now lives and works in suburban Northbridge, in the less-than-exotic county of Middlesex, and the only fiery passion you're ever likely to see there is on Friday nights outside the Kristos Kebab House, or in the bus shelter after the last bus has gone.

The old lady, who turns out to be American, replies in a voice like a lizard with laryngitis.

'Yeah, yeah, I know all that stuff, Mr DeBoulay, but as the late Mr Goldstein always used to say to me, "Never mind the art, Mamie, will it make money when we sell the damn thing?"'

Just at that moment, I spot Jade and her sister, Sky, across the room, talking to a right hooray with a spotty bow tie and a wine-coloured corduroy jacket. They look so completely babe-ular that it almost takes my breath away. Oh sure, Merlin, I really, really *am* over Jade' – NOT.

I haven't seen Jade for ages as she's been on an exchange with a French school and I'm wondering how she'll react to seeing me. After all, I did leave her alone at the party all that time back. It was the night I first kissed Lucy. She spots me across the gallery and waves with a big grin. Thank God for that. At least I'll get to talk to her again.

I look round the gallery and play a bit of famous-people-spotting. At the far side, underneath a portrait of what looks like one of the Queen's corgis, is that podgy bloke with the glasses called Trevor something, who does all the arty stuff on Channel 2, and there's that dodgy bird, who I saw in the papers – the one who managed to convince everyone that her scaggy unmade bed was art. Art schmart! I say. Oh yes, and there, underneath the portrait of himself, is Julian Clary, dressed like something off the top of a Christmas tree.

'Hello, Joe.' (*It's Jade.*) 'I'm really glad you're here. We never did get to talk and things at Mum and Dad's party. I'm really sorry, you went off to the loo. I met someone I knew and . . . well, you know.'

Yeah, I so do bloody know. I don't *belieeeeeeve* it – it seems as if she didn't even realise that I'd had a mega snogfest with Lucy in the garden. I don't quite know how to take that. I suppose the good side is that she thinks that *she* abandoned *me* – or is it?

'What do you make of all this, Joe – bit different to Northbridge, eh?' she continues.

'You're not kidding. Hey, Jade, I've always wanted to ask you or Merlin why your dad still lives out there? I'd have thought he could afford somewhere really groovy and posh even.'

'Oh, I don't know. Mum says he bought the house when he was only just beginning to make money and then, being a lazy old git, never got round to moving. Anyway, I think he rather likes being a big fish in a small pond. To tell you the truth, Dad can't stand these artsy-fartsy people for more than a couple of hours anyway.'

'Thank God for that. Have you spoken to Julian Clary?'

'Yeah, a minute ago. He's different; he's a right laugh

and dead gorge. Shame he's gay – what a sad loss to womankind.'

Looking at Jade I realise that she'd be a great test for gaydom. I saw a programme once that said that being homosexual got you out of fighting in wars, and lots of guys tried to use it as an excuse. I reckon they should have paraded somebody like Jade up and down in front of the naked men – that would have sorted the fibbers out good and proper (if you know what I mean). With high heels, she's nearly as tall as me and has on a long, black dress, a bit like her mum's (only using about half the material). Normally she wears hardly any make-up, but tonight it's obvious she's on the pull – with even darker than usual eyes and the reddest, shiniest lips I've ever seen. I can hardly believe I've actually snogged 'em.

Oh bugger, it's all happening again. I'm sinking like a love-sick brick in a bucket of pink blancmange. Jade has a way of looking at me that seems to go through my eyes and right into my brain (and then straight down to my trousers). Oh Lucy, where are you when I need you most?

I feel a tap on the shoulder.

'Hi there, Joe, we mentioned your friend Merlin's name on the door and hey presto – here we are. Hope you don't mind, sweetie.'

I whip round and it's cowboy Rik-with-a-k and Douggie, the two guys from the pub in Soho. Christ, what a bloody nerve – they've followed us.

'Oh, er – yes – um this is Jade, Merlin's sister. Jade this is – um – Rik.'

Jade takes one look at the heavily-denimed urban cowboy and then at my expression.

'Hello, Rik. How do you know my boyfriend? He's never mentioned you.' She slips her hand round my waist and touches my lips with an admonishing finger. 'You're a dark horse, Joe, the things you get up to when my back's turned.'

Is this girl brilliant or what!

It was time for Rik-with-a-k to look slightly embarrassed. He'd obviously assumed I was a sure-fire home-owner (as me and Merlin call gays).

'Oh, I'm sorry, I didn't – um – realise you were sort of ... Ooh look, there's Julian Clary over there. I simply have to meet him.'

Douggie, guessing the plot from my expression, winks at me and, with a camp giggle, follows his friend into the throng.

'Really, Joe, I see I must keep a closer eye on you,' Jade whispers.

'Don't blame me, blame your brother. I thought we were just going into the pub for a beer and we nearly came out with bloody husbands.'

'Don't tell me, Joe – this pub, was it in Old Compton Street?'

'Yes, I think it was.'

'You really should get out more. Everyone knows most of the pubs there are gay these days.'

'Do you think Merlin knew?'

'Too right he did. Did he choose?'

'Yes, come to think of it.'

I look across the room and see Rik-with-a-k all over Merlin like a cheap frock. Merlin looks at me desperately but I mouth back at him, 'Serves you bloody right.'

Jade then asks me if I wouldn't mind going out the back with her to see if her sister, Sky, needs a hand opening bottles. We go through the door but Sky's not there. She must have taken some wine back out to the gallery.

'This is in case you ever think too much about men,' she giggles, and snogs me just like she did at the wedding. I think about Lucy for a brief second and then don't. Look, it really isn't my fault, honest.

I come out from the back room in a complete daze. Any illusions that I'm over Jade have gone straight down the pan. How can I ever face Lucy again? I know some blokes can run a few girls at a time, but not me. I can tell porkies like the best of them, but not for long, and not without eventually being caught out big-time. But I'm still not sure what Jade wants of me. As far as I'm concerned there are four ways of looking at it:

A. She really fancies me and doesn't care that I'm over a year younger than her.

B. It's all just a game and she's simply enjoying the power she has over me.

C. She sort of fancies me but doesn't want it to go any further.

D. She simply doesn't think about it at all and just

reacts on the spur of the moment.

I stand in a corner for a bit to get my breath back and try to think logically. Let's examine the four alternatives. For a start I really don't believe in A. Jade Labardia could get practically any bloke she wants (except Julian Clary) so why bother with a sixteen-year-old (just!) schoolboy. B's possible, but knowing her family, I just don't think she'd be that ruthless. Besides, I do think she really likes me. C is more than possible, but now part of me thinks that she's the sort of girl that if she really wants something, would just go for it and bugger what anyone else thinks. D is by far the most probable. Merlin once said that she and her sister Sky play with men like toy soldiers, standing them up and knocking them over as the mood takes them. Just before I met Lucy I decided to act as if I really didn't care either way. This annoyed Jade admittedly, but it didn't really do me any good either. What's the point of keeping your pride in place if it means you still don't get the girl, eh?

I come out of the daze and realise that Merlin is talking at me.

'Where the hell have you been? I've been looking for you everywhere. Thanks a bunch for leaving me with Woodie.' (He's the cowboy in *Toy Story*, if you didn't know.)

'Don't you mean Woodie-with-a-w?' I giggle. 'Serves you bloody right. You knew it was a gay bar you were taking me into.'

'Ah, yes, sorry about that. I just thought it might be a laugh.'

'Well I hope those two see the joke when they realise you're straight. Blimey, Merlin, blokes have been murdered for less than that.'

The rest of the evening gets predictably out of hand. Arty people and not-very-good-but-free wine obviously don't mix that well and as soon as all the pretentious conversations about art die down, the fun starts.

Merlin's dad Tony, flushed with success (and booze), makes rather suggestive comments to anyone in a skirt; Sky Labardia's seen getting about as friendly as you can get in a public place with the son of one of Merlin's dad's best customers, and yours truly has three more snogging sessions with Jade out the back. I can honestly say I'm right back exactly where I was after she kissed me the first time. Except it's worse – what the hell am I going to do about Lucy?

As for Merlin, the situation with Rik-with-a-k gets completely out of hand. It all starts when Merlin, despite professing to be in love, makes a pass at the gallery owner's rather plump daughter (for plump, read well-endowed, who seems to be game-on. Rik-with-a-k, who's by now a bit pissed, overhears the conversation and accuses her of trying to pinch his new boyfriend. Merlin, who by now, I should imagine, has had enough of Rik to last a lifetime, tells him to go forth and multiply (in far less words), which sends him right over the edge.

The next thing I see are the two doormen trying to subdue and extract a biting, scratching, swearing, spitting cowboy, while the horrified guests look on.

So much for art . . . with an A.

Scene 11

The Labardia house.
Monday 10.06 a.m.

ACTION:

At last the time has come to start shooting our film, *La Maison Doom*. I feel quite relieved on two levels. I suppose I *should* say that the main one is that it will be the climax to all the work Merlin and I have been doing, but if I'm really honest, it's because I'll be able to spend some proper time with Jade. I've hardly thought about anything or anyone else since the art gallery snogging session, even though I'm pretty sure she hasn't thought about it one bit. I can't even begin to think about poor Lucy – I feel so guilty. I managed to avoid seeing her over the weekend, by saying we had so much to do preparing the shoot, but I'm not ever so sure she believed me. Even worse, I can't tell anyone else about it this time (except perhaps Gran), in case it gets back to her. I mentioned it to Merlin, but he's so obsessed with Chloe that he hasn't enough brainspace for anything else – apart from our film, that is. She's still away in France, apparently, but they've been text messaging each other like it's going out of fashion.

Merlin and I have written a full shooting script and are ready to roll. The action is supposed to take place in Paris in the 1950s, and we've managed to get the

72

Labardias' next-door neighbours to park their ancient Citroën 2CV van (one of the ones with the crinkly sides) outside in the drive to make it look a bit more French. Merlin's made a temporary sign on his computer saying: *Henri Leblanc – Taxidermiste, 17 rue St-Denis, Paris* and stuck it on the side of the van.

The first scene starts off with Tony, Merlin's dad, sitting in the window of their house surrounded by all the stuffed animals and birds that we've borrowed from Merlin's dungeon.

We've decided to shoot the film in black and white, because it looks older (and more arty). I position myself outside with the camera, so that when I zoom in on the first shot we'll just be able to see the van to one side. Merlin's dad, sorry – Henri Leblanc – can just be seen through the glass, wearing a huge black moustache and a beret, working on a large, dead, tabby cat (whose name had once been Lionel).

Next we see Madame Leblanc (Merlin's mum, looking surprisingly normal) walking in to be framed by the window. She appears to be jolly upset and is standing by his table pleading with him about something or other. Monsieur Leblanc stands up angrily, waves his scalpel around and then bashes her over the head with the cat before sitting down. He then carries on stuffing as if nothing's happened. (Good name for a blue movie – *Carry on Stuffing*.)

Merlin runs over from the house. 'How did that look? Could you see everything?'

'Yeah, I think it looked pretty groovy,' I reply. 'I'm not sure he should be hitting her with the cat, though – it's a bit much. You know what cat lovers are like.'

'Oh, that's all right. Lionel was a vicious old bastard, anyway. He probably would've enjoyed it. Anyway, we can't allow minority interests to curb our creativity.'

I can't believe he just said that.

The next scene takes place in the kitchen where Madame Leblanc, now looking all straggly and poor, is trying to feed two little toddlers, Mireille and Francine (also borrowed from next door), who are pretending to cry because their mean old father won't give their mum enough francs to buy proper food. We'd managed to make them look dirty and snotty, which their mother, almost understandably, got a bit stroppy about.

Monsieur Leblanc strides into the room, which also has had to be changed to look French.

'What are you whining about, woman?' he shouts in a not-bad French accent. 'Can't you shut zose childrens up?'

'Zey are 'ungry, Henri, zat is why zey cry. Zey have only had thin cabbage soup for three days.'

'Bah! Zey are lucky. It's good for zem. Why, when I was zeir age I used to dream of cabbage soup. Anyway, it is all we can afford.'

'But you always 'ave meat and bread and wine, it is not fair.'

'I must keep my strength up to earn ze money. You would have me going short? Would you? WOULD YOU? *WOULD YOU?*'

He grabs a wooden spoon and starts beating her over her head and shoulders while the children continue to howl (this time for real – much to their mother's distress).

There are a couple more scenes like this to establish what a total bastard Monsieur Leblanc is – her pleading for more cash to buy food and him drinking himself stupid and beating her senseless when given half a chance. Get the picture?

The next scene takes place at Northbridge Cemetery in the pouring rain. It's Madame Leblanc's funeral day. We've all gone there in Mr Labardia's brand new Range Rover and next door's clapped-out van. There's a bit round the back that's really overgrown and dead spooky. Monsieur Leblanc is with the two girls, Jade and Sky (who are supposed to be Mireille and Francine grown up), dressed in really short, home-made, French-style school uniforms with little straw hats. To be honest, they still look too sexy for my liking (who am I kidding?) and a bit too much like the older girls in the St Trinian's movies. It's awful. I can't seem to take my eyes off Jade and find it difficult to concentrate on the job in hand. Suddenly, poor Lucy comes into my brain and I start to feel guilty again.

Anyway, beside them, at the grave, is a friend of Merlin's dad's, dressed as a French priest and swinging about one of those thingies with incense that pour smelly smoke all over the place. Merlin's in the background, done up like an undertaker (his favourite fantasy), in a top hat and long, black cloak. He's borrowed a large, black horse from the riding school down the road, but nobody can quite see why – especially when it starts pooing everywhere.

They've just pretended to bury Madame Leblanc, who'd finally killed herself because of the way her horrible husband treated her. After Merlin's dad's friend has finished a few lines of mournful, unintelligible pretend-Latin, the camera goes right into the girls' faces who, after wiping the tears from their made-up-to-look-red eyes, throw their father the horriblest sideways stare for a split second. It's supposed to sort of predict what's going to happen. By the way, we've found some really miserable French-sounding accordion music to go with it.

'OK, everyone!' I shout when it's finished. 'It's in the can.' (Directors always say that.) 'Thank you very much, you were all brilliant.'

Jade runs over to me looking really excited.

'This is so cool, Joe. How do you know how to do it? You're so clever.'

'I don't really know what I'm doing, to be honest. I'm just hoping it comes out all right. At least I can see what's going on in this little screen by the camera. You and Sky look really good, by the way.'

'Aha, you like me in ze petit French school uniform, eh, *monsieur?*' she lisps, with an innocent, little-girl-lost expression and kisses me on both cheeks like they do in France.

I gulp, lost for words, and suppose I must look pretty stupid.

The following day, we decide to shoot the next few scenes which show the girls, now young teenagers, working alongside their father in the taxidermist's shop. We indicate time going by, by pulling off the pages of a calendar like they used to do in old American black-and-white movies. After a few years or so they become almost as good as him. Merlin's mum, who's now dead, of course, and out of the picture, turns out to be a wizard at make-up and making costumes, and is able to transform Mireille and Francine in stages from being small schoolgirls to beautiful young women. We'll sort of merge them together later on, in a kind of swirly, arty sequence.

As the years go by, the greying Monsieur Leblanc becomes very proud of his daughters, but has no idea of their evil plan to pay him back for the way he treated their mother.

As I'm going through the plot with everyone, I keep meeting Jade's eyes. She has a way of looking at me with just the faintest smile that nearly takes my breath away, and sometimes I completely forget what I'm talking about.

'OK,' says Merlin, 'it's time for the murder scene. Dad, we need you at the kitchen table, eating your supper.'

Monsieur Leblanc proceeds to munch the baguette, cheese and pickled onions we bought at Tesco. The two girls, as usual, have to prepare and serve him his food. Mireille pours him a glass of red wine and then winks evilly at her sister. Suddenly, Merlin's dad tears at his throat, falls across the table and lets out a bloodcurdling, gurgling scream. Unfortunately, everyone in the room bursts out laughing.

'CUT!' shouts Merlin, looking seriously pissed off. 'Come on, you lot, this is supposed to be a murder scene, not a bloody panto. You two girls can look sort of pleased, but not as if you're in a Jacques Tati film. It's beginning to look like *Monsieur Hulot's Holiday*.'

After about three more takes, Monsieur Leblanc finally manages to die without everyone falling about giggling and we all heave a huge sigh of relief.

'God knows what it's going to be like when the girls really get murdering,' says Merlin. 'I think we'll have to clear the bloody set.'

'What about the seduction scenes?' I say quietly. 'I can't imagine us all sitting through them with straight faces either.'

Jade throws me a look which leaves little to the imagination.

Just as I'm about to go, she calls me over.

'Joe, you wouldn't come up to my room for a sec, would you? I just wanted to go through what I'm supposed to be doing tomorrow.'

Jeez, this is the second time I've been invited. The

first time, at the party, I chickened out. I can't avoid it again – I'd look a right wally. I feel nervous and excited and guilty all at the same time.

* * *

I've never actually been in Jade's room before and have no idea what to expect. I look round in awe. If Merlin's room's whacky, then Jade's is from the same book, but not in the same way. It's done out like I imagine a rich Bedouin's tent would be. Brilliantly coloured, draped curtains, with tiny mirrors, hang from the ceiling in huge, droopy loops. In the far corner there's a sort of bathroom section with a little fountain with water tinkling into a marble pool with real little goldfish swimming about. Huge cushions are spread everywhere and the floor is covered with cream-coloured sheepskins. Her bed looks like something out of the Sultan's palace in that movie, *The Thief of Baghdad.* (Her mum apparently got it from the set of a fifties musical called *Kismet* when it closed.) It's festooned with floaty, see-through curtains and has its own sort of roof with tiny, shining stars. There are a lot of those hanging chimey things that jangle every time you walk past or open a window. The whole place smells of joss-sticks and Jade. Talk about exotic. (Or do I mean erotic?)

'Blimey,' I say, lost for words, 'I feel like I'm on holiday somewhere really hot and abroad. How long did it take you to put all this lot together?'

'Oh, not really that long. Mum helped me with most of it. Do you like it?'

'Like it? I've never seen anything like it in my life. It's like a film set. Shame we can't use it in ours.'

Jade walks across the room.

'Sorry, Joe, I won't be a moment. I just have to get out of these awful clothes.'

Jade stops at a sort of curtained off area and starts taking off her rather plain movie costume *on this side*, as if I'm not there. I try to turn away, but there are so many mirrors in the place, I can't help glimpsing her wherever I look. Jade must know I'm watching and seems to be enjoying showing off. Christ! What a family! What a girl! What a body!

Snogging Jade must be like driving a highly-tuned sports car when you've been used to driving a family saloon. That sounds like I'm putting Lucy down, but I'm not. I haven't snogged that many girls, but it's fair to say that Jade could start a school. She uses her mouth and her tongue like no one else I've ever kissed. She can tease you, tempt you, reward you, dominate you and even punish you, as if the whole thing is just an expression of her larger-than-life personality. Don't get me wrong, Lucy's dead sexy and a good kisser, but compared to Jade, if it were a race, she'd be just another runner.

The trouble is, just as it's getting really steamy, I start seeing Lucy and begin to feel bloody awful. It doesn't take long before Jade picks up on it.

'What's wrong, Joe? You seem to be somewhere else.'

I decide that I've got to say something before things go too far.

'Look, I should have told you. I meant to at your dad's exhibition the other night. The actual truth is, I've got a sort of girlfriend and I feel a right bastard.'

'Is it that pretty little girl at our party?' she says rather patronisingly. 'She's gorgeous. I thought she was looking at you a bit strangely. Honestly, Joe, what do you do to us girls?'

I know she's joking, but carry on anyway.

'Look, I'm not sure how I think any more. Lucy – that's her name – seems to be making it all a bit too heavy-going for my liking. On the other hand, I think you're just playing around with me.'

Jade sits up, buttons her top and then looks into my eyes with that melting stare.

'I'm sorry, Joe, I feel a right cow. I do really like you, honest, but you're right, it's all a bit of a game to me. I'm a bit of a saddo really. I don't want to get between you and your girlfriend, it's not fair, and if it means we can't, well – you know – then that's tough shit. Mum's always telling me I should take things a bit more seriously.'

I look up and realise that by saying that it's made me more crazy about her than I was before.

'I don't know if I really agree with you, Jade. My old gran told me the other day that at our sort of age, we're bonkers to get too stuck into proper relationships. I'd really like you to meet her, she talks more sense than anyone I've ever known.'

'Merlin told me she's fantastic. I'd really like that. I love really old people, they're so cool.'

'All I do know is that I've got to sort the Lucy thing out before I can do anything else. It's only fair really.'

Jade holds my head in her hands and kisses me on the forehead. 'Now I know *why* I fancy you so much, Joe.'

Blimey!

Scene 12

The Kingdom of Joe Derby.
Monday 7.15 p.m.

ACTION:

I left Jade determined to come home and have it out with Lucy. I know I'm two-timing, but I just can't seem to help it. I decided I can't carry on fancying Jade, and not owning up. But how can I do it without her feeling she's being dumped? I know she is being dumped, but is there a way I can say it so that it sounds like she isn't? What a bloody mess! If I'd have thought I'd feel like this I'd have never got into it. Or would I? The truth is I still fancy Lucy loads, but not – if I were strapped down with electrodes connected to my nipples – as much as Jade. The trouble with Jade, on the other hand, is that, even after that brilliant snogging sesh, she still isn't offering anything long-term, she practically said as much.

But what am I banging on about? I thought I'd decided I didn't want anything long-term anyway. Or do I? If Jade rang up and said that she'd decided she wanted to be my full-time girlfriend, would that make a difference? Too bloody right it would!

I suppose it's the fact that she never ever, in a million, trillion years, *would*, that makes the whole thing exciting. I also suppose that what I said to myself at the party about a bird in the hand being worth more than two in the bush, might not be actually true. I mean, I've

83

now got one bird – Lucy – in my hand, but I'd still give anything to have Jade in the bush – so to speak.

I start to rehearse the phone call to Lucy. Hang on, isn't doing something like this on the phone a bit wimpy? Gran told me that you should always do things face to face. The trouble is, I can't handle all that emotion. Knowing my luck, I'll say what I've got to say, then Lucy'll cry, then I'll give her a cuddle, then we'll have a snog, and then before I know it, we'll be back together again – as if nothing ever happened. If I could just say what I've got to say and run away, it would be all right, but that's a bit of a no-no I suppose.

It's no good I've got to do it on the phone. Mum and Dad have gone to see *Runaway Bride* or something equally soppy at the church hall, so I can use the phone without being overheard. I decide it might be an idea to try my speech out on Rover, so I sit him up and slap him about a bit to make sure he's paying proper attention.

'It's like this, Rover. I really like you ever such a lot, but I'm just not really ready to go steady.'

No response.

'But if I *was* into going steady, you'd be exactly the sort of dog – sorry – person I'd go steady with. I think you're really great.'

No response.

'I'm sure there are millions of guys who'd really love to have a girlfriend like you.' Oh hell, this is sounding so bloody patronising (and just a bit perverted).

Rover isn't convinced either and starts licking his bottom.

Hell's bells, this really isn't going to work, is it? Perhaps I'd better do it tomorrow. Yes, that's right – it's Tuesday tomorrow, far better for this sort of stuff.

I hear the phone ringing downstairs. That settles it – it's bound to be Merlin wanting to talk movies. Ha ha, saved by the bell.

I pick up the phone.

'Hello, is that you, Joe?' It's Lucy. (Bugger! Bugger! Bugger!)

'Oh, er, yes it is. Is that you, Lucy?'

'Is it all right to talk? I've got something important to say.'

'Er, yes, I suppose so. You sound very serious.'

'Look, Joe, I won't hang about. It's about us. I don't think we should go out any more.'

Wow! Did she just say what I thought she said?

'Really?' I say, in a state of shock. 'Er, why? I mean, what makes you say that?'

'I've decided that you're not ready to have a steady girlfriend. I like you ever such a lot, but I reckon you've still got a lot of growing up to do.'

'Hang on a min–'

'No, hear me out, Joe. I think that you should be seeing girls like Jade Labardia. They sort of serve you right in a way. She seems just like you – not exactly immature, but not ready or able to offer anything long-term to anyone else.'

'That's a bit heavy, isn't it? I thought you said I wasn't like all the other boys.'

'I know I did. In a way I now think you're worse. At least most boys might appreciate having a girlfriend like me. *You* don't seem to. *You* don't even remember my second name half the time. Anyway, I've thought it through and talked to Mummy. Look, Joe, I've got to go out, I can't talk about it now, I'm too upset. Anyway, I've made up my mind.'

With that the phone goes dead in my hand and I stand motionless for what seems ages.

It gradually sinks in. Christ Almighty, I've just been dumped. I, Joe Derby, have been well and truly dumped. There was me worrying about dumping Lucy and making her feel bad, and she goes and dumps me, before I get the chance to even reply. I'm supposed to be the *dumper*, not the *dumpee*! What did she say? Not ready to have a relationship? What bollocks! It's all right for me to say that, but not her. Rover looks up at me with a classic I-told-you-so expression on his stupid, hairy face.

'Who does she bloody think she is?' I shout at the poor dog. 'Just because I don't want to settle down and play stupid mothers and fathers right this minute. I wonder what she's doing now? I've a good mind to ring her back or go round there. Anyway, it's bloody cowardly to dump someone over the phone. Hey, I bet she's found another bloke. Yes, that's it! It's nothing to do with me being immature – she's found somebody else. Who do you reckon it is, Rover? I wonder if he's with her now – snogging in her room, on that bed, with her mother coming in and out. Damn, damn and bugger.'

I feel really miserable. I'm back to square one. I've blown it with Lucy and Jade's only playing with me. All I've got is Rover . . . and now he's farted – bloody brilliant!

I ring Merlin.

'Merlin, you'll never guess what's happened.'

'Rover's won the lottery?'

'I've just been dumped.'

'*You've* just been dumped! I thought it was *you* that wanted out of the whole thing.'

'She beat me to it.'

'Oh well, at least she saved you the trouble – welcome back to bloke-world. Nice to have you on board again, Joe.'

'She said I didn't know how to treat a girl.'

'Treat a girl to what?'

'Look, be serious. This is the first time I've ever been dumped.'

'Tough shit! I've never even got to a position where I could be dumped. Chill out, you'll get used to it.'

I could see I wasn't going to get a great deal of sympathy from that direction. Poor old Merlin still can't persuade Chloe to go out with him, so why should he commiserate with me? I decide to say goodnight and sleep on it.

Life, eh!

Scene 13

ACTION:

I hardly slept a wink last night thinking about Lucy and Jade, the two women in my life. But, knackered as I am, we have to film the stuffing of Monsieur Leblanc.

When I finally arrive, Merlin, Jade, Sky and their parents are waiting with the camera and lighting set up. A huge leg of pork and a big dish full of disgusting-looking liver and kidneys sit ominously on the table. Jade and Sky think it's a right laugh and can't wait to get stuck in, but I must admit to feeling a bit squeamish.

I'm doing the camera again for this scene, so I get everybody in position, talk them through the script with Merlin and shout 'ACTION'. The first shot involves the girls' 'dead' dad lying practically naked on the kitchen table with the two sisters wearing striped butchers' aprons and sharpening a couple of very scary-looking carving knives.

'Zis will teach him a lesson, Mireille,' says Sky. 'We'll see how *he* likes to be stuffed.'

'Ze biggest sing we've ever done before is a parrot, Francine, 'ave we got enough stuffing to fill 'im up wis?'

'Oh *oui*! Plenty. Papa had fresh supplies delivered ze day before yesterday. Let's get on wis it.'

I focus on Jade's lovely face and then allow the camera to wander down her shoulder (carefully avoiding her boobs), then her arm, along her hand and then, slowly but surely, to the knife and on to the tip of the blade. Meantime, Tony Labardia jumps off the table and puts the leg of pork where he's been lying. By focusing really closely on the point of the blade it looks just as if it's going into *his* skin. Gross or what?

Unfortunately the cut looks so realistic that my head begins to swim. After the take I whisper: 'Blimey, Merlin, isn't this a bit *too* flipping realistic?'

'No way, José, it's brilliant, let's get on to the bit where they pull his innards out.'

I won't go into the gory details, but by the time the shot's finished, both Jade and Sky have got pig's blood up to their elbows and are looking well pleased with themselves. We run it back on the monitor and everyone agrees it looks as if poor old Monsieur Leblanc is on his way to wherever bad taxidermists go.

'Jesus, this makes *The Silence of the Lambs* look like "Blue Peter," says a rather shocked Mr Labardia. 'Are you sure you want it so real? Bloody good job it's in black and white.'

'Course we do,' says Merlin. 'Anyway we can always tone it down in the editing if we have to.'

We then do the old fade-out technique to imply time marching on and then I pan in on the last stages of the leg of pork being sewn up. Mr Labardia climbs back on the table and his wife Jane, Merlin's mum, paints stitches all the way up his side. From a distance they look identical to real ones. Poor Monsieur Leblanc looks well and truly stuffed.

'Right then,' Mrs Labardia says, lifting the mutilated leg of pork over to the oven. 'If you're finished with this, I'll pop it in to roast. It should be ready by supper time. Waste not want not, I always say.'

It's funny, but everyone pulls a slight face at this suggestion. Maybe it's having been used as a substitute for Mr Labardia, makes the idea of eating it smack slightly of cannibalism – like eating the stand-in, in a way. It reminds me a bit of *Zombie Flesh Eaters* a rather daft horror film I saw once.

When we stop for a break, Jade takes me to one side.

'How did it go last night, Joe? Did you manage to speak to Lucy?'

'Er, yes, it's all sort of settled.'

'Well done, there's a brave boy. How did she take it? Was she upset? I hope it wasn't too gruesome.'

'Er, a bit, but I explained that she and I would never work and she seemed to accept it.'

(Look, I know I should have told the truth, but that wouldn't really have helped anything. Anyway, nobody wants someone whose just been dumped, do they?)

Jade pats me on the bum and says in a quiet, sexy French voice, 'Well, Joseph, I sink you deserve a great big reward for that, *mon chéri*. You must visit my little apartment again soon. I'll see if I can find you somesing nice.'

Jeez!

Scene 14

The Labardia house.
Wednesday 11.00 a.m.

ACTION:

When everyone is assembled in the room we've made into the taxidermist's workshop, we begin to shoot the next scene. Jane Labardia, Merlin's mum, has done a wicked job with her husband's make-up, transforming his rather healthy, Italian colouring to deathly pale, with two rather obvious and heavy-handed-on-purpose pink patches on his cheeks. He really does look like a corpse who's been made up to look real – a bit like Michael Jackson on a good day.

I start filming just as the two naughty sisters begin arranging him to look as if he's working on one of their ex-rabbits. I almost have to pinch myself to remember he's not really dead. Brilliant stuff! It's now time to bring in the cops.

The next bit of the story goes like this.

For months now, the two sisters, Mireille and Francine, have been placing their dead father in the window of his workshop every morning. (They keep him under the table at night.) To the casual passer by, on the other side of the net curtains, it looks as if he's still alive. Meanwhile, the two girls carry on the taxidermy business as usual in a back room, telling their customers that their papa is too busy to see them.

One day, a handsome young *gendarme* (that's me folks) passes by on his rounds and notices that the insurance on their Citroën is out of date. (Jane Labardia, by the way, has managed to adapt a French policeman's outfit borrowed from a company in Northbridge specialising in male strippergrams.)

He knocks on the door and waits until Sky appears. He then asks to speak to her father, the owner of the car. Sky tells him he can't talk at the moment because he's sick. Unfortunately, before they'd had a chance to remove the body, the policeman had spotted him 'working' in the window. He begins to smell a rat (or a dead dad).

Realising the game could well be up if she doesn't do something fairly drastic, Sky invites him into the drawing-room and leaves him with Jade while pretending to go and talk to her father. When she comes back, the two of them set about seducing him. Oh, by the way, although they now hate and detest all men, they realise they still have their uses (well, one use in particular!). The big plan, therefore, is to have their wicked way with the poor young policeman and then, while in a state of undress, murder him. What a way to go, I can't help thinking.

Merlin becomes the director for this bit and his father operates the camera. The two girls, both dressed in remarkably fanciable fifties gear with pointy bras, tight sweaters, ponytails and ribbons, invite me (the *gendarme*) to sit down on the sofa. They take it in turns to tell (between sobs) how their poor father has been a recluse since their mother died, and how desperately poor they are.

If it isn't bad enough having Jade practically sitting on his lap (my lap), Sky then places her hand on my knee and starts massaging my leg. Oh blimey, it's all starting again – mass movement in the trouser department (and it's not my truncheon either!). What is it about these sisters? Don't they know I'm a happily married *gendarme*?

I can just see out of the corner of my eye that Jade has spotted my panic and is smiling knowingly. She then puts one arm round my neck and slips her other hand inside my shirt. Hell, one Labardia was bad enough, but now they're both at it . . . I can feel myself going redder and redder and my collar beginning to feel like it's about to burst. Just as I'm about to explode, Merlin yells: 'CUT! . . . Brilliant! Joey boy, you were bloody fantastic. I never knew you could act – you're a bloomin' natural. I thought for one second you really were going to faint.'

I really do mean to tell him I'm not acting, honest, but it just comes out as, 'Oh well, I, er, well, it's just a question of mind over matter really.'

'I didn't think this scene was going to work,' Merlin rattles on excitedly. 'I reckon we should press on while it's going good.'

'I thought the rest of the seduction scene was going to be off camera,' I say nervously.

'So did I, but hell, man, it looks so convincing, I think

we should carry on at least till it's about to get really heavy.'

Everyone else agrees and I'm completely outvoted.

The following scene, I'm sorry to say, will remain stamped in my memory for ever – and then some. The two girls, now well into their parts (and mine), start nibbling and licking my face and neck and massaging my body all over. It's all a bit like the *Emmanuelle* films I used to sneak from my dad's shed. As all this is going on, my mind suddenly returns to Lucy and what she'd say if she could see me now.

It's by far the sexiest thing that's ever happened to me times a hundred and I feel myself losing control. Jade and Sky, of course, know exactly what effect it's having on me and are loving every moment. Eventually, just as I'm about to scream, they get up and pull me, shaking like a leaf, to the door which leads to the bedroom (as was originally planned). Thank the Lord, I thought for one moment they were going to rape me in public. As the door closes behind us, Merlin shouts 'CUT' again and everyone cheers.

'Fantastic, terrific! Blimey, that was brilliant,' Merlin shouts, as we come back into the room.

That evening we all sit round the kitchen table to eat the remains of Monsieur Leblanc (or should I say the leg of pork). We've looked at the video footage and, though a bit rough in parts, we all agree it is pretty cool, all things considered. I could hardly watch the seduction scene for embarrassment. Let's face it, I knew I wasn't acting.

'Poor Joe,' says Mrs Labardia. 'You looked as if you didn't know what to do with yourself. As for you girls, where did you learn all that stuff from? Not from me or your father, that's for sure.' Mr Labardia then throws her a very knowing wink, which we're not supposed to see.

'Oh, you know, Mum,' Sky giggles. 'We've read all about it in books. Why – did it look convincing?'

'Convincing?' cries Mr Labardia, 'I reckon you two could run a school for blue-movie actresses.'

'Now there's a job,' yells Merlin. 'Can I be the headmaster?'

'Are you all right, Joe?' asks Mrs Labardia.

'Just about, thanks. I would have preferred not to have had to do the second bit.'

'Ooh, Joseph darling, don't you like us two leetle French girls?' Jade says in a dead sexy accent. 'We thought you might be almost enjoying eet.'

Just as I'm beginning to go red again, their mother breaks in.

'That's enough, girls, leave poor Joe alone. I'm sure neither of you could have coped if it had been the other way round.'

'TRY ME, TRY ME!' they both yell in unison and we all fall about laughing .

So much for girls!

The Labardia house.
Thursday 5.30 p.m.

ACTION:

This morning's filming was a riot. Our mate, Spike Adams, who's always looked quite old for his age, and a bunch of fairly big guys from year twelve, arrived to play the next procession of policemen who turn up at the house.

Here's the next bit of the plot.

After the two girls murder me (the first policeman), they stuff me and hide me out the back. We were pleased we shot the old leg-of-pork operation from several angles as it meant we were able to use the footage again (without emptying the local butchers and having to eat blinking pork for the rest of our lives).

Anyway, after a couple of days, a detective comes to the front door asking if either of the girls have seen the young policeman. He was observed by an old lady, just down the road, walking past her house. By the way, we're going to shoot the police station scenes later, when we can find a place that looks like one.

When Mireille and Francine realise that the new cop is also getting more than naturally suspicious, they ask him (that's Spike this time) to come through to the drawing-room. Poor Spike copes even less well than I did with the seduction scene, hardly resisting at all, and the girls, looking slightly shaken, have to drag him through to the back before *he* starts ripping *their* kit off.

'CUT!' screams Merlin. 'Spike, what the hell are you playing at, you cretin? You're supposed to be a respectable married detective – not a raving sex maniac. The idea is that you're trying to resist their advances, not to jump on them. Jeeeesus! This movie's going to be X-rated if we're not careful.'

'Sorry, Merlin, but you try acting cool with all that going on. It's dead easy for you – they're your sisters.'

And so the story rolls on. As each new policeman turns up, the two French girls, now really into it, drag them through to the back, have their way with them and kill them. In the end they have to stuff them with anything they can get their hands on – old clothes, straw, newspapers – you name it. Gradually, they begin to run out of spaces to hide the bodies, so they hit upon the idea of placing them round the dining table with their ex-dad at the head. It all begins to look like a scene from the old horror classic, *Mystery of the Wax Museum* in which the mad sculptor smothers his victims in wax to make them look like exhibits. Poor Mrs Labardia has had to work overtime adapting costumes and making my mates up to look dead, but she seems to love it. I can just imagine my parents doing that sort of thing – NOT!

I suppose the plot, now I come to think of it, **is** rather unlikely, but you can get away with a lot in films that you can't in real life. Anyway, the filming goes surprisingly well, all considered, and at the end we feel fairly sure that it will hang together pretty well.

When we've finished and had a cuppa, I hang around after the other guys have left hoping that Jade will invite me up to her room as promised.

She doesn't. Dammit!

Scene 16

The Kingdom of Joe Derby.
Thursday 6.30 p.m.

ACTION:

It turns out Jade's going out this evening, so I'm left to make my sad way home. I hope life's a bit more exciting when I'm a proper movie director. With a bit of luck I'll be going to premières and award ceremonies most nights after work, knocking around with all those dead gorge starlets, all trying to outdo each other by seeing how little they can wear without being arrested (or molested). I used to be able to talk about this sort of thing with Merlin, but all he seems to do at the moment is moon about in a sort of dream. He told me the other day that he's not looked at another girl since meeting Chloe (until I reminded him about the girl at the art gallery). Anyway, all he does now is send Chloe text messages every ten minutes. It's all a bit nerdy.

As soon as I get to my house I sense something's wrong. Dad's car's in the drive much earlier than usual and, as I let myself in, Rover stays in his basket and looks balefully up at me. Something's up! Mum walks straight out from the kitchen as she hears me come in. Her eyes look as if they're red from crying. I wonder if she and Dad have had a row.

'Joe, darling, I've got something awful to tell you. Come into the kitchen, sit down and have a cup of tea.'

My mind races. What could it be? My sister Zoe's left Graham? No, that's not very terrible . . . blimey, that would almost be top of the *good* news. I know, Dad's been made redundant. Actually, when you come to think of it, that's not that too bad either.

I go into the kitchen and Dad's sitting there looking like he's just won the lottery but lost the ticket.

Mum says, 'There's been a loss in the family, Joe. We're all very shocked. We know it will mean a lot to you especially.' I search Mum's face and she nods. Oh hell, it can only mean one thing. There are only two people in my family that I really, really care about and one of them's in his basket.

'When did it happen?' I say, fighting to keep my voice from wobbling.

'It was this afternoon. She had a massive stroke. The doctor said she didn't feel a thing. They found her slumped in her chair with the remains of a cigarette in her fingers and a half-drunk Guinness by her side.'

I nod slowly and turn to walk up the stairs to my room in a sort of daze. Rover slinks after me at a respectful distance. I enter my kingdom and fall on the bed. I'm not ashamed of crying – *honest*, but my eyes are dry. In a way I wish I could.

I only saw her a couple of days ago. Me and Merlin went over as we do every few weeks, to see if we could do anything in her little garden – cutting the hedge and mowing the lawn – that sort of thing. She'd made us a brilliant tea and we'd told her all about the film.

Shit, shit, shit – I can't believe it! My dear old gran, probably the only person that really understands me in the whole bloody world (apart from Rover) – dead. Shit! Bugger! Sod! Damn! Bugger! Shit! Bum!

Rover jumps up beside me and looks as if he almost knows what I'm thinking. I throw my arms round him and hold him so tight that he begins to struggle as if I'm suffocating him. Oh, hell's bells, she's the first person who's died that I really ever cared about. OK, there's been the odd distant uncle or aunt, and two years ago Mrs Armitage, the two doors away neighbour's wife, got mown down by a milk float (embarrassing or what!) but Gran was part of my life. She should at least have stuck around until I was grown up.

'Are you all right, dear?' It's Mum outside the door. 'Do you want to talk?'

I try to speak but the words don't come.

'We'll be downstairs if you want us, darling.'

'Thanks, Mum,' I manage to squeeze out.

I imagine my old gran, fag in one hand, drink in the other, sitting laughing in her chair. Why of all people did she have to go? Why couldn't it have been stupid Great-Uncle Harry? Nobody would miss him – silly old sod. I look up at the wall and spy a little photo of Gran, me and Rover, taken at Swanage last year. Suddenly from deep inside I feel this sort of pressure, coming right up from my stomach, into my chest, through my throat and into my head – like I'm about to boil. It's no good, I can't help it, my eyes are starting to stream. Suddenly a huge sob shakes my whole body just as if someone's pulled a bloody great lever. The floodgates open and I cry like I've never cried before. Poor Rover, not knowing quite what to do, begins to howl. Suddenly, I see my dear old gran, looking down over her glasses at the scene and begin to see the funny side. The next minute I'm howling too – with laughter . . . and then crying again.

I look up and see that my dad has come into my room, probably for the first time in years. He sits down next to me on the bed. Oh no, not another lecture – please Dad, not a lecture on being grown-up and responsible and all life having a beginning and an end and all that crap – not today.

'I can't begin to know how you're feeling, Joe,' he almost whispers.

'Your gran loved you more than anyone else in our family. She always thought I was far too staid and boring, which I probably am. She always loved me of course, and she was a wonderful mum, but . . . I used to envy you – my own son – because I knew she was such an amazing woman and she loved you best.'

I look up, tearfully, but in pure astonishment. He's never said anything remotely like this to me before – ever.

'I know what you think of me, Joe, but you must understand I do really love you underneath it all. It's just that I'm different . . .'

Then, for the first time I can ever remember, he puts an arm round me. I turn and throw my arms round him and sob like a kid. After a minute or so I look up and see he's crying too. *MY DAD'S CRYING TOO!* Christ Almighty, my old man's bloody human after all. What a shocking thing to find out when you reach sixteen.

'I thought you might like this,' he says in a gentle voice, and then stands and quietly leaves the room. I look down. It's a miniature bottle of brandy. Shit, man, this is almost too much to take in one hit.

Rover goes back to licking his balls. That's dogs for you.

I wait until my parents are safely plugged into 'Coronation Street' before I sneak to the phone.

'Hi, Merlin, it's Joe. Can you talk?'

He's got his own phone in his room so usually can.

'Sure, Joe, how's it hanging? Everything OK? I thought the filming went fantasti–'

'Sorry, could you shut up for a minute, I've just had some bloody bad news.'

'Don't tell me, Zoe's preggers.'

'Even worse than that.'

'Graham's preggers.'

'My gran's just died.'

Total silence for a few seconds.

Merlin's voice again, only quiet and shaky this time.

'Sorry, man, that's bloody awful. When did you find out?'

'When I got home from yours. It had just happened, apparently.'

'She was so cool, your gran. Are you all right?'

'Better than I was, thanks. I had another shock though, just after.'

'Christ, what this time?'

'It's my dad.'

'He's not dead too?'

'No, you stupid prat. My dad came into my room and was completely brill; it was really weird.'

I told Merlin exactly what had happened.

'Jesus, that's like finding out Adolf Hitler was really quite a nice bloke underneath it all.'

Trust Merlin to say the wrong thing at the right time. I laugh and it feels a bit better.

'I just didn't realise my dad felt anything. I just thought that all he cared about was his job, his golf and being a regular member of toytown (my favourite expression for being straight-laced).

'You'd be surprised. You never know, things might get better now. Stranger things have happened. Anyway, what goes on now? Is there going to be a funeral?'

'No, Merlin, we're going to take her on a bloody skiing holiday. What do *you* think?'

'Can I come, please can I come?' Merlin sounds really excited.

You'd think he was trying to gatecrash a party.

'Only if you'll help me make it something special that everyone will remember for ever.'

'Something that your gran would have really approved of. Boy, what a brill idea, Joe. Like sort of immortalising her. We could even video it. That's about as cool as you can get. Why don't you come over, we could talk about that and finishing the film.'

'OK, give me ten.'

Somehow doing something makes me feel a thousand times better.

Scene 17

The Labardia house.
Thursday 7.30 p.m.

ACTION:

Merlin's waiting in his room-cum-dungeon-cum-pet funeral parlour when I pull on the bell-rope outside his room. After he's checked me out through the little inspection hatch in the heavily-studded dungeon door ('borrowed' off a film set by his dad), he lets me in. The room is reassuringly the same – dark as a *Hammer House of Horror* film with the eyes of all the ex-pets glinting in the flickering light of the dozen or so candles.

'Want a cuppa?' he asks, strolling towards the little kitcheny-bit far away in the gloom of his huge room (one of the perks of a rich dad).

'Cheers, mate – two sugars.'

'So, what shall we do at your gran's funeral?'

'I don't know, but whatever it is, we mustn't upset anyone. It's got to be cool and something she'd have approved of.'

'I've been thinking, why don't we tell everyone that some well-known film star's going to be there – a long-lost relative or something? That way we'll have thousands of people. It might even get on telly.'

'Yeah, but there'll be a riot when he or she doesn't turn up.'

'What about doing it like the Oscars, awarding your

gran a kind of lifetime achievement award, like they do? Only this time it's a sort of *after*life award.'

'If I had my way we'd hire a magician to make the coffin disappear or something.'

'I don't think your rellies would go a bundle on that,' Merlin giggled. 'Let's think. You and I *could* go as angels and hover on wires over the coffin.'

'Come on, Merlin, be serious. No, whatever it is we do, we must make everyone really sad that she's gone. I think we should make a little film of her life.'

'Why don't we sleep on it?' Merlin replies. 'Let's talk about *La Maison Doom*.'

'Yeah. We haven't really worked out a good ending yet.'

'It probably should have someone discovering the table with all the stuffed men round it.'

'Like who?' I ask.

'How about the window cleaner?'

'Brilliant! I hardly think they'd be having the windows cleaned with six stiffs in the room. Anyway, they'd have drawn the curtains.'

'Hang on. Why don't we flash forward to the modern day? Tell you what, we could shoot the last bit in colour to make the point, like they did in *Raging Bull*, do you remember? The two girls will then be old and wrinkly, like the old dears in *Whatever Happened to Baby Jane?*, and the whole house will be like a real creepy old museum.'

'You're a very strange bloke, Merlin, but it's better

than anything else so far. But how can we actually end it?'

'OK, let's see. A young journalist comes round to write about their strange work. They turn him away for ages, but, because they are secretly proud of their skills, they eventually let him in to show him the best pieces they've done throughout their lives . . . But who can we get to play him?' says Merlin. 'Tell you what, I'd like to have a bash.'

'You'll have to do something with your hair, you don't get that many French journalists with blue dreadlocks.'

'How do you know?'

'OK,' I chip in, not prepared to argue the point, 'when he's actually in the house, they decide to have one more go at a human – to fill up the very last seat at their father's table, which has been empty all those years. It'll be their life's work completed, sort of thing.'

'Unfortunately, their female charms don't work that well any more, and the young guy gets suspicious,' Merlin adds, 'so he comes back in the middle of the night and forces the dining-room window. He looks in and is so shocked that he lets out a slight scream which wakes up the old ladies.'

'I've got a better idea. Why not have the old dears standing in the candle-lit room as if they're serving drinks to the corpses?'

'Brilliant! . . . And then, the very last scene could be a loony-bin somewhere outside Paris, where they've been sent. It could be a bit like the one in *One Flew Over the Cuckoo's Nest*.'

'Even better. We do an outside shot of somewhere that looks as if it could be a loony-bin and then show the old ladies in it. The audience will assume that they're the inmates, but it turns out they're just visiting.'

'Who?' says Merlin.

'The young journalist, who they find white-haired and jibbering in a corner of his room.'

'. . . from the shock of the scene. Fantabuloso! Hey, partner, I think we've got ourselves an ending.'

Genius, or what!

Scene 18

Gran's funeral, St Mark's Crematorium.
Tuesday 11.30 a.m.

ACTION:

This is the second time my family's been thrown together in just a few months. Although I don't really go in for churches or most of the stuff that goes on in them, I have to turn up at the crematorium, for my dear old gran's sake, if nothing else. This time, however, I've got Merlin by my side – in the same outfit that he had on in our film – without the top hat (or the horse . . . of course).

'Tell me who's who?' he whispers, as we all gather outside the gloomy little chapel waiting for the last lot to come out.

'Where shall I start?'

'Who's that old guy over there, waving his arms about and looking like the fat bloke in *Oliver Twist*?'

'Mr Bumble,' I whisper.

'What a stupid name.'

'No, you muppet, that's the character in *Oliver Twist*. The bloke over there's my great-uncle Harry.'

I glance across to where Great-Uncle Harry, looking absurd in a long, black frock coat, is spouting off to one of my distant aunties. I lead Merlin over so that we can catch what he's saying.

'Believe me, my dear, I've never had a day's illness in my life,' he lies. 'Clean, honest living that's what I put it down to. And, of course, hard work and a clear conscience. You mark my words, my sister wouldn't have been where she is now, if she'd listened to me.'

I feel like shouting 'BOLLOCKS' at the top of my voice but manage to restrain myself.

'But surely, Harry, seventy-eight is a fairly good innings,' replies the auntie – a rather grey, saggy little woman who looks as if she's spent far too long at things like this.

'Seventy-eight! That's nothing. Why, I'll be eighty-one next August and look at me. I tell you, it'll be some illness that manages to put me under.'

'I'm amazed no one strangled the prat at birth,' mutters Merlin under his breath. 'What a pompous old fart.'

'I tell you, mate, I might still be the one to do it yet.'

Merlin looks round the gathering crowd. 'Any babes about?'

'Blimey, Merlin! It's a bloody funeral. You don't reckon you're going to pull here, do you?'

'Oh, I don't know. Can't think of anywhere better. At least everything's going to seem jollier after this – even me.'

'Hang about,' I say, 'I thought you were swearing undying love to Chloe. You made out you didn't even notice other girls.'

'Yeah, well, it's always good to have a reserve team. Hey, who's that over there?'

'Who, the one with the big . . .?'

'Yeah! Jesus! She's awesome, man.'

'That's my cousin Clare. I must have told you about her.'

'You never did, you spasmo. Keeping her, or should I say *them*, to yourself, were you?'

'You're joking,' I reply. 'I tell you, her boobs are very much her best feature – she's real pants when you get to talk to her. Anyway she's my cousin.'

Merlin wasn't put off.

'Why should that worry someone as deeply shallow as me? How can I get to talk to her?'

'At the "do" after the funeral – after we've done our bit – I'm sure you'll find a way of bumping into her or *them*.

'Difficult not to in your house.'

I give him one of my withering looks.

'Just because you live in a Gothic mansion, there's no need to rub it in. If you had a do like this in your house, there'd be old rellies lost for days trying to find their way out.'

People are now pouring out of the chapel and I imagine the former star of the last funeral takes his final bow in the form of a thin column of blackish smoke hovering over the crematorium roof.

If it seems I'm making a joke of my gran's death, I'm not . . . just funerals. I don't buy all this soul-going-to-heaven stuff. Me and Merlin have talked for ages about what really happens when you die and can't believe all that stuff it says in the Bible. Reincarnation, though – that's another thing. Merlin, I'm convinced, really *would* like to come back as a werewolf or vampire or something spooky. Whizzing around in the middle of the night, searching for virgins, in a long, black, floaty, cloaky thing would be his idea of heaven (or hell). As for me, I reckon it would be pretty cool to come back as someone like Rover – sleeping all day, with nothing to get up for, being fed when you want and absolutely no chatting-up required with the lady dogs in the park. Woof woof, I say!

Joking aside, I just want to remember my gran as she was – laughing and being rude and smoking too much and drinking too much and taking me seriously when no one else did. As far as I'm concerned, what's in the coffin that's being carried into that chapel, is just an empty body in a shiny box. Anyway, apart from all that, I don't need some weird ceremony to remember my gran by. I'll never forget her . . . ever.

We fall in behind my literally 'great' auntie Hilda as she nearly gets stuck in the little side door of the chapel on the way in.

'Blimey, you could hold this funeral in a tent if you used all the cloth in that coat,' Merlin whispers, forgetting how loud your voice always carries in this sort of place.

'Did you say something, young man?' Auntie Hilda bellows, whirling round and nearly knocking us off our feet.

'I said there's a lot of froth in the moat,' replies Merlin brilliantly, if somewhat obscurely.

The room turns out to be a tribute to pine. There's so much pale wood in the place that it looks more like one of those Swedish sauna thingies than anything churchy. A rather gawky young bloke wearing a vicar's outfit comes in from the back room. He looks like it might be his very first gig by the way he's hopping from one foot to the other.

'May I extend a w-warm and h-hearty welcome to you all on this sad but somehow joyful day. As you know we are g-gathered here together to remember and celebrate the life of . . .' he takes a sly peak at the programme and reads, 'Ada Derby – who sadly passed away, and is leaving us this day for her final journey to heaven to spend eternity with the Lord, our Father.'

Merlin farts quietly, accidentally on purpose, and I do my best not to giggle. Everyone looks at everyone else to see who did it. If my gran could have seen all this she'd have hooted out loud – wherever she'd been.

'Now, l-let us pray.'

Nobody ever really knows what you can get away with and what you can't in this sort of situation. My great-uncle Harry and great-auntie Hilda and a gaggle of the other older rellies, make a right production of falling to their knees to show everyone else how holy they are, while the rest of them half-sit, half-kneel, half-close their eyes in a sort of embarrassed attempt at piety. I stay bolt upright, but soon feel the inevitable slap on the neck from my mum who's right behind me.

After some long-winded stuff about holy ghosts and eternity, the vic announces the hymn – 'God How Great Thou Art.'

A funny-looking little organist, who looks as if he's just come in from mowing the crematorium lawn (and his hair), launches into some obscure tune, that I swear nobody has ever heard before. That doesn't hinder my great-uncle Harry, who bellows the incomprehensible words in his horrid, wobbly, syrupy voice, without bothering to use more than three different notes. There really is no worst sound in the world than a smallish group of random English worshippers who don't know the tune, singing at the top of their dreadful voices.

By the time we've finished the prayer/hymn routine, with everyone bobbing up and down like ducks on a pond, it begins to resemble a sort of Christian musical chairs.

I close my eyes and see my dear old gran slipping me that little special wink that she always did at formal occasions when we both found something funny that we weren't supposed to.

At the end, when the vic's blessed practically everything but Auntie Hilda's massive bum, the little curtains part and the coffin begins to roll back. I can hardly bear to look.

'Looks more like she's being sent to hell, poor old thing,' whispers Merlin. 'What a waste of all those brass handles and hinges.'

'Someone told me they whip them all off. They've apparently all got deals with the local coffin-makers.'

'Cool. If they were even quicker they could tip whoever's in it out and get the coffin as well.'

Audible shushing from behind.

Suddenly, from out of the blue, there's a loud clap of thunder. Merlin and I look at each other, then towards the heavens and waggle our hands in the air, as if to wonder whether it might be God's way of telling us to shut up too.

When we get outside everybody seems to be saying to everyone else that they hope that they'll meet under better circumstances next time. I must admit that the last time, Zoe and Graham's wedding celebrations, weren't exactly 'much better circumstances', but I dare say some of them, particularly Zoe and Graham might disagree.

I turn round and see a familiar sight waddling towards me.

'Oh no, Great-Uncle Harry Alert!' I whisper.'
Too late, he's seen me.

'Ah, young Joseph, caught up with you at last. A wonderful send off and an excellent turn-out, I think you'll agree. Your grandmother would have been well-satisfied, young man.'

'I don't think she'd be that well-satisfied with being dead,' I mumble under my breath but, as the old twerp never listens, it goes unnoticed. Merlin hears, however, and nearly wets himself.

'As for me,' he continues, 'I must say,' (he MUST say), 'when I finally am called to my maker, I don't want no fuss nor bother, but I expect all the good folk of my home town will have something else to say about that. I'm rather afraid they'll turn out in their droves whether I want it or not.'

I really feel the need to assure him that there probably won't be too much fuss made when he finally pops his clogs. If the good folk of his home town feel anything like our family, they'll be glad to see the extremely large back of him. There could even be dancing in the streets.

Just then I catch a glance of my sister, Zoe, with her dreadful husband. Have you noticed that there are some women who, as soon as they've trapped their man and got the old gold ring on the finger, change completely – for the worse. In less than a few months my sister has managed to age twenty years – middle-aged hair, middle-aged clothes, middle-aged handbag and a sort of resigned-to-having-to-listen-to-her-boring-husband-prattling-on, middle-aged way of standing. As for Graham, any fears that married life might cause him to shape-up (or shut-up) seem well out of the picture. He's beginning to look like a sausage that someone's tried to shove too much meat in.

'Crikey, what's happened to your sister?' whispers Merlin. 'I used to fancy her rotten. Now she looks as if she's had one of those magazine make-overs . . . only back to front.'

'That's life with super-stud, Graham, for you. She's probably knackered on account of his astonishing performance.'

We both look at Graham and burst out laughing.

The funeral blokes are waiting by their cars, chain-smoking impatiently. One of them is hopping mad because he's just picked up a parking ticket (I bet my dear old gran would've found that hilarious). They obviously want to whip us lot back home smartish so they can get on with the next lot.

'I wonder how many funerals they get through in a day?' I say to Merlin.

'As many as they can, I should think. I bet they hate us standing around yapping though. They could end up having to do 'em two at a time.'

At that moment there's another thunderclap and it starts to tip down, causing everyone to make a mad dash for the cars. Mum and Dad have already sped off home to whip the cling film off the pork pies and sandwiches and stick the sticks in the little sausages, or whatever you do. Dad, true to form, managed to get his hands on a case of sweet sherry, cheap from the closing-down sale of our local off-licence. When they've got through that, he'll serve up the fruit punch that he always insists on making.

While Merlin and I had been trying to work out ways of cheering up what looked like it would be a dismal affair, we'd both remembered Laura's barbecue in the summer, the one where Laura pepped up the 'teenage' punch with a bottle of her dad's vodka (and Merlin got shown the door for grabbing her boobs).

Now, Merlin and I have never been much cop at science, I admit, but we did pay extra attention during the lesson on alcohol and how and where it comes from. We spent many a long evening experimenting in Merlin's room with bits of equipment 'borrowed' from school until his dungeon looked like the laboratory in *The Man With Two Brains*, (my favourite Steve Martin movie). The end results were admittedly disappointing, but we did produce a cloudy liquid that, although tasting fairly yucky on its own, certainly gave a kick to anything else, providing the flavour was strong enough to annihilate it.

While Dad's out in the shed, having a 'secret' fag, I slip a Coke bottle's-worth in the punch to help it along a bit. Bad move number one, Joey boy!

But the main feature is yet to come. Merlin and I have spent the last few nights preparing the little video starring my gran. Mum and Dad had sorted us out a whole suitcase of photos, mostly black and white, going back to when she was a baby in the twenties, and even before. Using Merlin's dad's kit, we managed to transfer them all on to video with little clips of old cine-film thrown in. I suppose, when I think about it, I did it more for myself than anyone else.

'Ladies and gentlemen,' my dad announces, 'if you

could go through to the lounge, Joe and his friend, Merlin, have made a little programme as a final tribute to his grandmother.'

There's much ooing and aahing amongst the rellies, but when they all finally settle down, Merlin fires up the video and my commentary begins.

'Ada Louise Tilbrook, my gran, was born above a small grocery shop in the Roman Road in the East End of London in the winter of 1923 to Herbert and Amy Tilbrook.'

We show a picture of Herbert and Amy outside their shop with my gran in her mum's arms and what must have been Uncle Harry (who was a fat little bastard even then) standing with what looked like a teddy bear but could have been a limp puppy.

'Aah yes, that's me all right,' he butts in. 'We might be smiling there, but we had it hard in those days believe me. Why, I remember the time . . .'

Everyone, in chorus, much to my delight, tells the old fart to shut his silly old face (in not so many words).

'From an early age,' my voice continues, 'she was the comedian of the family, always playing practical jokes and getting into trouble. There was one time, she told me, when she and her little friend tied some strong cotton between the door knockers of two opposite houses further up their narrow street (photo of street). When the first person came to the door and opened it, having heard a knock, it pulled the cotton taut, lifting

121

the knocker of the door opposite, (three second footage of door knocker). As that person came to their door, the first lady had just closed hers so the whole thing happened again. This went on five or six times, until the two neighbours, well-cross by now, sussed they'd been well and truly had.'

As the video continues, Mum and Dad keep serving the fruit punch to our audience, who by now are holding up their glasses for more, which is slightly unusual.

When we recorded the film, I found I could remember nearly every story that my grandparents ever told me, including the one about my grandad's pet monkey, given to him by his brother who'd brought it back from the war in Africa. It apparently chased Gran down the street and that was how they met. But Gran, so the story goes, soon made him get rid of the monkey – it was her or him. (I reckon my sister would have chosen the monkey.) Then there were the stories of *her* grandmother who had seventeen kids, only four of whom survived. One particular one, I remember, was about little Ernie who climbed the wall of a carpet-beating factory at the end of the street and was dragged into the machine by one of the huge revolving hooks. No trace of him was ever found. I used to love that story.

As I'm watching with the others, I can actually hear Gran's dear old voice and it makes me very sad. I can remember the long evenings I'd spent as a little kid, sitting by Gran and Grandad's fire in the front parlour of their weeny house listening to tales of their younger days. My sister, Zoe, always thought them boring, but for me they made the past seem alive.

By the time we get near to the finish, I'm so upset I can hardly stand it. It hadn't seemed so bad when we were making it.

Our little show ends with a short clip of film, the last ever taken of Gran, outside a pub at Swanage, the year before last, with a pint of Guinness in her hand, a fag in the other and laughing her head off. The room's now totally silent and, as I look round, practically everyone has tears in their eyes – even Merlin, who's been momentarily diverted from my cousin Clare's boobs.

Dad gets up and walks straight over to me and Merlin and, seemingly lost for words, stares us straight in the face and formally shakes both our hands. I think it's the very first time I've ever done anything that he's been remotely proud of.

'I don't know about the resht of you,' he eventually gets out, 'but I for one will treashure this little experience for the resht of my life.'

Merlin and I look at him closely and realise he's showing all the signs of being as pissed as an alcoholic newt.

'That goesh for all of us, hic,' splutters Auntie Hilda, tears streaming down her face. 'By the way, Derek, is there any more of that delishush punch?'

Dad totters over with another jug of punch, tripping over the rest of my rellies, who all seem to be in a similar state.

Great-Uncle Harry stands up shakily and waves his empty glass about.

'I'd like to propose a toasht to my late shister, Ada, who unfortunately cannot be with us today.' He looks round for approval but when there isn't any he carries on: 'Here's to my sishter Ada, who unfortunately cannot be with us today.'

Then my funny little Auntie Doreen stands up. She's never been known to say boo to a goose, but this time she excels herself.

'Sit down, you old piss-head. You've said enough to last us a bloody lifetime.'

With that she swings her handbag, knocking the old fool back in his chair.

I look across at Merlin and point to the door. He casts a final, sad look at Clare's chest and gets to his feet. When we're outside he almost dissolves with laughter.

'*You* didn't put any of that stuff in the punch, did you?'

'Yes,' I reply, 'we agreed I was going to.'

'No, you moron, we said I was going to.'

'Oh shit, does that mean . . .'

'Yeah, let's get the hell out of here, Joey boy.'

I hesitate for a couple of seconds.

'We can't. We've got to stick around to make sure no one drives home. We can't have them all ending up in the nick.'

Luckily most of my rellies live locally and can leave their cars. The others are told in no uncertain terms by

Mum, who knew better than to touch the punch, that they have to get cabs or stay over. She convinces them it was the really strong sherry that Dad served when they arrived, but I can tell she isn't fooled one bit. My short period of favour with either her *or* Dad will, I fear, soon be well and truly over. Still, the most important thing is that we not only did something that my gran would have appreciated but by spiking the punch, managed something she'd have found dead funny too.

Bye, Gran. We'll miss you.

Scene 19

Northbridge High School.
Wednesday 10.30 a.m.

ACTION:

After the funeral yesterday, I suddenly felt really alone. It wasn't just that I'd never see my dear old gran again, but I was missing Lucy badly. I really wanted to talk it through with someone, and I know she would have been on my side. I'm beginning to realise what I've lost.

Merlin and I somehow didn't manage to get back to school after the service. Funny that! We ended up going round to his place to start editing our film instead.

The last couple of scenes had gone pretty well, though I say it myself. Merlin, though not completely convincing to me as a French journalist, made a pretty cool, white-haired loony. Anything that gives him a chance to change his hair colour always seems to get him going.

It has to be said, the scene where he climbed through the window to be met by eight corpses sitting round a table with Jade and Sky looming in the background practically scared me to death, even though I was one of the stiffs! Unfortunately, Jade and Sky, despite old ladies clothes, glasses, grey hair, no make-up apart from age lines, and severe failure in the standing-up-straight department, still managed to look like babes, which we all decided we had no choice but to live with.

Making those two look ugly was like trying to make Sylvester Stallone pretty.

We shot the asylum scene in a ward of the local hospital. Merlin's dad had donated some money a couple of years ago to help the drug dependency unit, so they owed him a favour.

'Do you think we should end the film in the asylum, or should it be just the two old dears shuffling home?' I ask Merlin.

'If I had my way, I'd have made a mad dash and murdered them on the spot with my bare hands, but no one seemed to go for that.'

'Too obvious. I think the audience should be left guessing until the last minute. The final take should be Jade and Sky hobbling out of the asylum grounds. We could shoot that in the park.'

'OK, maybe you're right.'

Jeez, I think – that was easy.

We're actually going over it in double Maths, my least favourite subject. Merlin, despite himself, is actually quite good at all that sort of thing, but I'm useless to the point of hopeless. I just can't seem to get round the logic of it all. Worst of all are those stupid problems that go like – 'If it takes seventeen one-armed Irishmen seven weeks to dig a hole twenty-five metres deep, how long does it take an ostrich with a blunt beak to bury its head in a bucket of cement?'

'Mr Derby, are you still with us? I hope I'm not

interrupting something important. You seem to be somewhere else?'

It's old Ma Dixon our Maths teacher. For some reason, she has always had a go at me. They never talk about that when they go on about bullying at school. I'd like to tell her that I'm daydreaming about snogging my ex-girlfriend, but I have a feeling it might not be appreciated.

'Would you be kind enough to tell the class the answer to y equals x squared?'

'Er, I . . .'

'Would I be right in supposing that you haven't a clue what I'm talking about? Please inform us all about what a quadratic equation actually is.'

I stare blankly at her, trying to remember what they are.

'Come on, Derby, the rest of the class are all waiting to share a sample of your vast mathematical knowledge.'

'I have a feeling they might be something that I'll never need to use,' I say quietly.

The class titters, but I realise it could be a bad move.

'I beg your pardon? I didn't quite hear that.'

I repeat my answer.

'If your knowledge and application in Mathematics is anything to go by, Mr Derby, there must be hardly anything you'll ever need to use. In which case your brain must have more vacant capacity than anyone else's in the school. A condition which is becoming abundantly clear.'

Blimey, she's turning into Anne Robinson.

'Thank you,' I reply, well aware it was an insult.

Talking about brains. There's something about my brain that point-blank refuses to have anything to do with Maths. I always wonder whether my total lack of interest comes from not being able to do it or whether not being able to do it causes my total lack of interest. Either way, the old bag's beginning to get on my tits. You don't find people getting their heads torn off because they can't draw, or act, or run fast, or play musical instruments or flipping skateboard for that matter, but everyone seems to be on your back if you can't do bloody sums.

'So, Mr Derby, you don't think you might actually *need* some knowledge of Mathematics?'

It's old Ma Dixon coming back for the kill. She's now pushing too hard. All sorts of warning bells go off in my head. If she carries on riding me much more I know I'm going to explode, and that won't be a pretty sight.

'Only enough to work out how much money I'll need to buy a calculator,' I mutter under my breath.

The class erupts in nervous laughter.

'Sorry, I didn't hear you. Am I becoming hard of hearing, or have you been struck dumb?'

Oh no, here I go. RED ALERT! I can feel it. I'm beginning to bubble over. This must be what murderers feel like just before a crime of passion. It's only happened a few times before, and each time I lost it completely. Merlin sees the signs and begins to look nervous. He grabs my arm and tries to put his hands over my mouth, but it's too late.

'Look, Mrs Dixon, I might not know what a quadratic equation is exactly, but I do know lots of other stuff and I'm only sixteen. If you're so clever, how come you're still working in a dumb school like this? Before taking the mickey out of me maybe you should take a long look in the mirror.'

A stunned silence falls over the whole of the class.

Mrs Dixon looks as if someone's just surgically removed all her blood and then eventually speaks in a quiet, trembly voice.

'I think, Mr Derby, a visit to the head teacher might be in order. No one has ever spoken to me like that before in all my long career. Leave my class this minute and wait outside Mr Earnshaw's office. I'll be along at break. You'll be sorry you ever spoke to me like that, young man. Very sorry indeed.'

Strangely enough Mr Earnshaw, our new head teacher, quite likes me. He knows that I can work really hard at the things I'm interested in and, much more to the point, I helped push his car single-handed, when it conked-out outside the school gates only the other day. I reckon he just might owe me one.

At break I have to endure standing next to old Ma Dixon while she tells the boss word for word what I said and what a wicked influence I am on the class.

'Thank you, Mrs Dixon, I'll deal with this now. You go off and have your break.'

'I hope you're going to discipline him to the limits

of your power, Mr Earnshaw. We can't have this sort of thing in our school.'

'Thank you, Mrs Dixon – as I said, I'll deal with this. Now, please leave us.'

As she strides out of the room muttering away to herself, he comes round to my side of his desk, looking dead stern.

'Now – er – Joseph, this is very serious. I can't have you talking to my staff like this. I understand that you had to go to the funeral of your grandmother yesterday. Has that got anything to do with your lack of control?'

'No, sir, nothing at all. It's just that riding me like she does, never does any good. I try my best, but Maths just isn't my thing.'

'We still can't have that sort of behaviour in class. Otherwise it could turn into a battleground.'

My mind flashes back to the fifties movie, *Blackboard Jungle*, about a schoolmaster who completely loses control. I suppose he has a point.

'So what am I going to do with you?' he continues. 'I have to be seen to punish you quite severely, otherwise there'll be anarchy in the classroom. I'm afraid I'm going to have to deprive you of something you really like for a while. What can it be? What do you enjoy most? I bet you're fond of sport – football and everything – most lads of your age are.'

'Yes, sir,' I lie fluently. 'I live for football and cross-country running.'

He walks round the room with his hands clasped behind his back.

'Well, I'm sorry, Joseph, but I have no choice. I am going to have to ban you from all games for the rest of the term. You're going to have to stay inside. I'll apologise to Mrs Dixon on your behalf and ask her, as delicately as possible, to leave you alone. As you might know, she will be retiring at the end of this term, so you won't have her for much longer.'

I hang my head in mock shame.

Good old Earnshaw. I know for sure he's not stupid. I bet somewhere along the line he's heard about Merlin and me, *Les Deux Slobbinos*, and our notorious efforts to get out of anything to do with sport.

'Thank you, Derby, that will be all. You may go.'

As I'm leaving I turn round and catch him trying his best to cover a smile.

When I get out to the playground, there's a small crowd waiting for me.

Merlin gets to me first.

'Blimey, Joe, you were awesome, man. What did he do? Have you been kicked out?'

'Much worse,' I reply, trying to look heartbroken.

'Jesus, what?' says Spike Adams. 'Is he going to haul you up in front of the whole school and make an example of you?'

'Much worse.'

(I'm loving this, by the way.)

'Hell, Joe, what is it? – he hasn't called your old man in, has he?'

'You're not going to believe this, but the old bastard's banned me from sport for the rest of the term.'

Total silence breaks out as the penny drops.

'You jammy old bullshitter,' Merlin cries, grabbing my jacket. 'How in hell's name did you swing that?'

'Earnshaw worked out what I'd miss most, and I owned up. As you all know, I cannot tell a lie.'

And that's a lie . . .

Northbridge High School.
Friday 11.00 a.m.

ACTION:

Actually, life would be all right if I didn't feel like shoving my head down the toilet every time I think about Lucy. My mate, Spike, never known for his timing, told me that, according to his impeccable sources, she was going out with someone else. I'm so glad that she's happy – not! Thank God we've got *La Maison Doom*.

Word had got right round the school about our film. Mr Grange, head of Art, calls Merlin and me into his room. We quite like old Grange the Strange (as we call him), but he does have a tendency to take life a bit too seriously. His idea of a fun night out would be something like a visit to a gallery of some obscure, abstract artist followed by a new-wave poetry-reading session.

'Ah, Joe and Merlin, I've been hearing stories about a film that you've just made. I was wondering if it might be suitable to show to our sixth-form film society. We could do a special evening and open it up to whoever else wants to come. I doubt whether there'll be many – there never are. Could you tell me roughly what it's about?'

We describe *La Maison Doom* very loosely, so as not to give anything away and old Grange still seems to like the idea.

'Ah, yes, it sounds rather like some of the early French, postmodern Gothic films I used to follow at university. I must admit I'm very impressed. It's about time someone did some serious work in this place. Can you make next Thursday after school? We were supposed to be having *Battleship Potempkin*, the Russian classic, but I've been let down. Could you design me a poster I could put up round the classrooms?'

'Blimey, Merlin,' I say, as we leave the room, 'we're going to have to get our skates on if we're going to finish editing the bloody thing. I hope old Grange doesn't expect anything like *Battleship Potempkin*, it's a right grumpy old film.'

'Why don't we try to get a couple of days off? It is proper work after all.'

'Do you think we described it properly? I got the distinct feeling he thinks it might be all arty and stuff.'

'It is arty. I think it could be a sort of classic of its kind. They might even show it at the British Film Academy one day. We could be famous.'

I look at Merlin and realise he's absolutely serious. Oh well, I think, who am I to argue with my fate.

If fame is my destiny, who am I to deny it?

The School Hall, Northbridge High School.
The following Thursday 6.00 p.m.

ACTION:

Merlin and I have been working so hard on our film that we've hardly had time to worry about other stuff – like girls. The whole Lucy thing has gone as quiet as the grave and I'm feeling like yesterday's bread – still just about edible, but very much second best. I've now heard she's definitely going out with someone else, but my spies don't seem to know who (or are reluctant to tell me who the bastard is). Merlin's having slightly more luck. Chloe's back from Paris and, although she still doesn't want anything to do with him on a touchy/feely basis, seems happy to communicate on a higher level. This involves endless text messaging and long discussions on art, which isn't what's on Merlin's mind at all . . .

It's our big evening. Merlin and I can hardly speak we're so nervous . . . but not as nervous as Grange the Strange. He's jumping around like a mouse in a microwave. The poor bloke can hardly believe his eyes; the school hall is nearly full with kids and staff and with ten minutes to go they're still pouring in thick and fast – well not fast . . . just thick! I don't quite know why, but maybe it's because Merlin's posters look like they were designed for a porno/horror film. He used a still from the movie featuring Francine and Mireille looking gorgeous (*naturellement*), holding their bloody carving knives above their heads. I look round the hall to see if Lucy's here. I haven't even caught sight of her since she dumped me and I'd rather like her to share my moment of glory. But at least Jade is here with her sister, looking dead grown-up in her after-school clothes.

At six o'clock, a very self-conscious-looking Mr Grange walks to the front and holds his hands up for silence.

'Ladies and gentlemen, I'd like to thank you all for coming out tonight. I hope you've all done your homework.'

Pause for laughter.

. . . Silence.

'You are obviously all aware that two of our year eleven students, Merlin Labardia and Joseph Derby, have been working on their own film for some time now. We are very privileged to be the very first audience to see the result of their efforts, which I hasten to add, was only finished the day before yesterday. Even I haven't seen it yet, so haven't even had a chance to cut out the rude bits – ha ha! Their film is called *La Maison Doom* and as it progresses you might recognise quite a few other pupils from our school who have entered into the awesome world of drama to help our young film-makers. So, without further ado, could we have the lights down, and could you all stop talking when the film begins.'

'Here goes, Merlin,' I whisper, 'be prepared to run for it.'

Eventually all the coughing and sneezing stops and the titles begin to come up. Merlin's dad had the video transferred to 16mm film by one of his mates who runs a company that does that sort of thing. Merlin's opening graphics tend to lean more towards comics than serious cinema, but they still look pretty flash. Apart from the occasional splutter the hall is now silent.

For the first ten or fifteen minutes, as the story unfolds, the audience keeps pretty quiet. I look across at Mr Grange and notice that he has his serious-appreciator-of-the-arts face on. It's only when we get to the first operation bit that things start to hot up. There's a faint muttering heard round the hall and some of the littler kids start shuffling uncomfortably in their seats. When Jade and Sky start pulling out their dad's entrails, several of them have to be led out whimpering and every now and then comments like 'urgh' or 'gross' rise above the sound track. Old Grange starts looking nervously at the other staff members and at one stage they're making signs as if they're planning to shut us down.

It's only when the French sisters' father is put into the chair in the window that things start to go *not* according to plan. Having said that, what *does* happen turns out to save the evening.

Suddenly, from somewhere near the back of the hall, I catch a little giggle. It could have meant anything, but this leads to another from somewhere near the front and then one from the middle, until there's an audible build-up of suppressed giggling from an audience who don't know whether they're supposed to find the whole thing funny or not. They're most certainly not!

When it gets to where Jade and Sky are well into seducing me, just about everyone has decided it's a black comedy and are laughing out loud. Jade and Sky seem to be enjoying it too and when I catch Jade's eye, she gives me a big thumbs-up. Merlin and I, so's not to appear uncool, smile along with the audience, but underneath we're both dead cross.

By the time the young detective (i.e. me) is led off to the bedroom, everyone's literally crying with laughter. Even Mr Grange, who's tried his best to take it seriously, is now grinning from ear to ear.

By this time, you can hardly hear the sound track, kids are literally wetting themselves with laughter. As each corpse is sat in the dining-room a fresh wave overtakes the one that hasn't even had a chance to die down.

'Jesus, we haven't had the madhouse scene yet,' I shout to Merlin above the din. 'What are they going to make of that?'

'I can't believe it. Did you think it was funny when we did it?'

'Not at all, but I suppose, if you think about it, it does have a funny side.'

When Merlin, as the journalist, climbs through the

window and sees all the stuffed detectives (which is supposed to strike terror into all), it practically brings the house down. Kids are clutching each other and sobbing with laughter. Even the younger kids who were taken out, have crept in to see what they're missing. The teachers too have lost any form of cool and are laughing fit to burst.

I look round the hall and suddenly, before I can control it, I start giggling along with everyone else.

Poor Merlin, who's definitely not amused and who still considers this a serious work of art, has to hold a sort of wavy smile on his face to cover his puzzlement.

The last scene puts the tin lid on it. When the audience sees Merlin quivering in the corner of the loony-bin and realise what's happened, all hell breaks loose. I've never heard laughter like it at any film I've ever been to – ever.

And then it's the end. As the final credits roll up the screen, a huge cheer breaks out and everyone tries to fight their way to the front to slap us on the back.

Mr Grange, now red-faced and red-eyed from laughing so much, wades through the mayhem to the front again, mopping his face with a hankie, and waits for all the commotion to die down. He thanks everyone involved in the film, especially Merlin and me.

'Blimey, suddenly we're comedians,' Merlin says, as we're walking to McDonald's after the show.

'Maybe we went a bit too far. I must admit it did look a bit like *The Producers* in parts.'

The Producers, by the way, is one of our favourite funny films made by American film-maker, Mel Brookes. It's about two Jewish showmen who get people to invest fortunes in a Broadway show. The idea is that they'll put on a show in such bad taste that it'll flop after the first night and they'll keep all the dosh. The show, called *Springtime for Hitler*, is so outrageous and over the top that it becomes a massive hit and they lose out. I know how they felt.

'But we weren't even trying to be funny,' says Merlin, gloomily kicking a pile of leaves high into the air.

'That's probably why.'

'I thought it would at least *frighten* everyone. I reckon we're going to have to tell a few porkies otherwise we're going to look a right couple of prats.'

We get back to Merlin's house and meet Jade and Sky. They'd been at the show but slipped away because they were getting a lift home with a couple of the sixth-formers.

'Well done, you two,' Sky says. 'How do you like being famous? We didn't realise it was supposed to be funny. No one laughed that much while we were making it, or when we ran the takes.'

Merlin steps in right on cue. 'Oh that was all on purpose. We were trying to make it work on two levels. It was always supposed to be a comedy.'

'What was the other level then?' Jade asks with a hint of piss-taking.

'Oh, that was all the horror bit near the beginning. When people have been scared or made to feel sick it makes them really relaxed. They laugh at anything then – it's a sort of reaction. Isn't that right, Joe?'

'Er, sure, everyone knows that.'

'I'm not sure if it's going to do my future career any favours,' says Jade. She, like Merlin, wants to go on to drama college when she leaves school.

'Rubbish,' laughs Merlin. 'You probably won't even have to do an interview after that.'

'You're joking, I'd be lucky to get a job as the cleaner,' she replies with a giggle.

She could clean my drama college any time.

Scene 22

Merlin's dungeon.
Friday 5.30 p.m.

ACTION:

I've just called in at Merlin's before going home.

When we turned up at school this morning, just about everyone was going on about our film. All those that hadn't seen it were literally pleading with us to have another showing. I suppose this could be the nearest I'll ever get to being famous, and to be honest, I'm not sure I really like it. After you've said the same things a few times it becomes a bit of a drag. Imagine being *really* famous and having articles written about you in the *Sun* or *Hello*, or even having to go on chat shows every five minutes churning out the same old crap. And imagine people suddenly going quiet everywhere you go and gawping at you – whether you're walking down the street, or eating, or drinking. And imagine being like the Royals, with the world's press trying to get a quick snap of you doing anything – and I mean anything.

Merlin feels totally different of course.

'You must be mad, I'd love it. People hanging on to everything you say. Being able to get in everywhere for nothing – and what about all the girls you could have? They'd be lining up just to stand next to you let alone anything else.'

My mind turns to Lucy.

'Jeez, Merlin, if the last couple of weeks have got anything to do with it, one's going to be more than enough for me,' I say grumpily. I still can't get the fact that I've been dumped off my mind.

The phone rings on Merlin's extension.

As he listens, his eyes open wide and he begins to stammer.

'Er, really. Er, yes, of c-course. Er, when were you th-thinking of?'

Silence for a couple of seconds.

'Tomorrow morning would be very good for me. We, that's me and Joe – sorry – Joseph Derby, will both be here. Thank you very much.'

He listens a bit more, says goodbye, and puts the phone down.

'Blimey!'

'What? Why will we be here?'

'You're not going to believe it.'

'WHAT? I can't believe anything if I don't know what it is.' (Merlin can be really annoying at times.)

'You know that nerd Phillips in the lower sixth?'

'The one we call Where's Wally? – What about him? Was that him?'

'No, dickhead, I've just had his dad on the phone.'

'Who, Wally senior? Oh brilliant, what have we done now?'

'Nothing. Did you know he edits the arts page on the *Northbridge Gazette*?'

'So?'

'So, he said his son, Craig, came home last night going on and on about *La Maison Doom*. He wants to do an interview with us. He's coming round tomorrow morning with a photographer.'

Bloody hell! Me being interviewed for a proper paper. COOL or flipping what? Please forget everything I said earlier about being famous.

'Are we going to tell him the truth?' I ask.

'About what?'

'About it being meant to be a serious film.'

'Are you barking mad? Course we're not.'

'He's bound to ask where we got the idea from.'

'Easy, I'll work it all out tonight and tell you in the morning. Don't worry, our secret's safe with us.'

Famous last words.

The Labardia house.
Saturday 10.40 a.m.

ACTION:

I don't get to sleep until almost daylight, thinking about the interview today – so I'm late getting up. Only I could oversleep on my big day. By the time I get to Merlin's, Mr Phillips, the newspaper bloke, is already there and waiting to start. I haven't even had a chance to hear how Merlin's going to explain why and how we planned to write a comedy, so I'll just have to let him do all the talking.

'Right now, boys, let's start at the beginning. How long have you two been wanting to make a film?'

I can safely answer this one, so go first. 'We've been talking about films – especially old films – since we first became mates – er – friends. We both want to go into the movie business when we leave school.'

'Yes, but talking is one thing. How did you actually start? Most people wouldn't know how to begin.'

'You've got to have the stuff to do it with first.'

'Exactly, how did you manage that?'

'Well, my dad's an artist,' says Merlin, 'and he often works off stills from his video camera. He's now got most of the gear to shoot and edit films. I suppose we'd have had to have waited much longer if we hadn't been able to use it.'

'So whose idea was – er – what was it called – *La Maison Doom?*' Merlin gives me a let-me-do-the-talking glance. Here we go, folks – stand aside for Porkie Express.

'Well it all started with my family's pets. We've always had loads of animals and we like to keep them after they're dead to remind us, sort of thing.'

'Sorry, you've lost me. You keep all your dead animals?'

'Yeah, and all my relatives' pets too – my dad knows a guy in Islington who stuffs them.'

'Oh, I see, a taxidermist. Is that where the bear wearing the cowboy hat in the hall comes from? I take it he wasn't a pet?'

Merlin, the new hot-shot comedy writer extraordinaire doesn't realise it's a joke.

'No, we haven't had a bear yet . . . Anyway,' he continues, 'he gives him all our pets when they die – dogs, cats, even gerbils. I've got most of them in my room. Do you want to see?'

The bloke looks a bit flustered.

'Er – no, thank you, I'll take your word for it.'

'So,' Merlin says, 'we got this idea about stuffing actual people.'

'A strange subject for a comedy, don't you think?'

Merlin doesn't bat an eyelid. He's well into the bullshit now. It reminds me of the nonsense he dished out in the gay bar.

'We thought it was quite good. Nobody would *really*

stuff their father and then sit him at the head of a table with loads of other stuffed men.'

'Well, that's what I'd have thought. Do you like funny films best?'

'Not really. I'm into horror films – vampires, werewolves, all that stuff.'

Careful, Merlin.

'So why did you decide to make this a comedy?'

Merlin doesn't even blink.

'We didn't really have the right equipment for the special effects needed in a proper horror film, so we thought we'd start with something fairly simple – a spoof. You can get away with a lot more if it's not meant to be taken seriously.'

'A bit like pantomimes.'

'Er, sort of.'

Poor Merlin, I realise how much it must have crucified him to have his serious work compared to a pantomime. Even I'm not that thrilled.

'Well, according to my son it was extremely funny. Tell me, have you any plans to show it again?'

'Not as yet,' I reply. 'It's all a bit sudden.'

'I might be able to help. I know a few people in the entertainment world. Would you mind if I made some enquiries?'

Strangely enough, we say we don't mind a bit.

The interview goes on for about another half-hour. He asks about the other actors, our parents, our favourite films and lastly about school. I go on a bit about having to do a whole load of stuff I'm not interested in and Merlin tells him how boring we think most of the other kids are. The poor bloke looks a bit offended (on account of his son) and when he asks if we know him, I can see that Merlin's dying to burst in with his opinion. I manage to kick him under the table before he says a word.

The photographer takes pictures of me and Merlin in Merlin's dungeon, surrounded by all his dead pets. Jade and Sky, not wishing to miss out, come in halfway through wearing clothes that make even Merlin's eyes widen. They're both wearing their little French school uniforms, but this time with tons of make-up and high-heeled shoes. The poor old photographer who, I'm sure is only used to taking the usual stuff in local papers – mayors, old folks' homes and cats stuck up trees, starts to dither and go red. He even has to put the camera on a tripod to stop it shaking. Mr Phillips, who waited downstairs, and didn't see the girls, says he'll let us know when we're going to be in the paper, and that he'll try to find another gig for the movie. Cool.

'How did it go?' asks Sky, when they've finally gone.

'Easy-peasy,' says Merlin, 'I quite like all this interviewing business.'

'What about you, Joe?' asks Jade. 'What's it like to be a star?'

'Very funny. I don't really think the *Northbridge Gazette* is exactly the most influential paper to be seen in.'

'It's a bloody start though,' cries Merlin tetchily. 'You

wait, we'll have the people from colour supplements round before we know it.'

'More likely *Razzle*,' I joke, viewing Jade and Sky with much admiration.

'You wouldn't have us looking like boring old librarians, would you?' says Sky with a little jokey pout.

'No way, you and Jade are our secret weapons.'

I'd read a lot more if librarians *did* look like that.

Scene 24

The Kingdom of Joe Derby.
Saturday 6.30 p.m.

ACTION:

I really don't know where I'm coming from. There I was, driving myself bonkers trying to think of ways of getting Lucy off my back, and now I can't get her off my mind. It doesn't seem possible – one minute I had one of the best-looking girls in the school as my girlfriend, and the next she gives me the big heave-ho because I hadn't been giving her enough attention. What a prat! Merlin even had a go at me the other day. He said I'm just like a little kid that's bored of a certain toy, but as soon as another kid shows interest, wants it back again. That's rich coming from you, I said, and then told him to 'go away' (in different words), but when I really think about it he might have a point. I must admit that being dumped by someone certainly doesn't make them *less* attractive.

To make matters a trillion times worse, and maybe to prove Merlin's point, just as I was walking home from his place a couple of hours ago, I saw her driving down the High Street with that creep, James Burton, from the upper sixth. So that's who it is. He was in his dad's brand new, bright yellow, open-topped Audi, and she was laughing and looking totally babe-ular. Just as they passed me at the bus stop, she went out of her way to throw me one of those big who-needs-a-wanker-like-you smiles.

Why did I let her go? Why couldn't I just go along with it all like my mates do? Why didn't I realise at the time that just about all the other guys at school drool over her? Now I'm back to square one and it's all my own stupid fault. Even the girls in my magazines don't do the trick at the moment. I keep getting distracted, by thoughts of her.

I suppose before long I'm going to have to tell my mum and dad that me and Lucy are no longer an item. They've already started asking why she doesn't ring any more and I had to tell them that she's on holiday with her parents. That can't go on for ever – they're not stupid (well they are, but not *that* stupid). Jeez, I can just hear my mum prattling on about how often she'd told me that I didn't make enough of an effort; not to mention Dad saying crap things about nice girls like that not growing on trees and that anyway she was far too good for me. I've been hoping and praying that she'll phone me again to say that she can't live without me and stuff, or at least to give me the chance to talk my way back. I've even lay on the bed staring at her photos, willing her to pick up the phone, but that obviously doesn't work. The one thing I'm beginning to notice from my vast experience of girls (joke), is that once they've decided they're no longer going out with you, that's it – on to pastures new. We blokes do it different, I reckon. If nothing else comes along fairly quick after a split, we start looking back wistfully, remembering what we had. That's where I'm at now, sod it . . . wondering if I'll ever get a girl as good-looking as Lucy again, or if anyone will really like me as much as she used to say she did.

Maybe I *could* get her back if I really grovelled and made up some excuse. I mean, only a couple of weeks ago she said she was crazy about me. There must be a bit of that left. I know! I could say I was really broken up about Gran.

Suddenly, I imagine Gran wagging her finger at me from heaven (or wherever she went) and that makes me sadder. She wouldn't have me doing anything as wimpy or dishonest as that. Anyway, she hadn't even died by then. Maybe I could say that the film took me over completely and I had nothing left for girls. Not bad, but I suppose that doesn't exactly say much for the future. I mean, if I ever really *do* get into the film business I'll *never* have time for anyone, let alone her. Maybe I could just tell the truth (makes a change) and say that I didn't realise how great she was until she'd gone. Play the sorry-I'm-a-silly-bastard card.

Anyway, I'm sure if she's been going out with James Burton she'll have to appreciate me again one day, he's such a git.

But how shall I do it? I know she thinks I'm quite cool-looking and so it had better be face to face. Anyway, I'm never that great on the phone, so I'd be starting way down the field. I think we'd better meet on neutral territory. Maybe after school. No, that's no bloody good, I'd be in school uniform. How cool is that! That'd put James Burton at an instant advantage. Sixth-formers can wear what they damn well like. Why's life so unfair?

I ring her number and a female voice comes on the phone. It's her mum (sorry – her mummy).

'Is Lucy there, please? It's Joe.'

'No, I'm afraid she's gone out with a friend, Joe.'

(Yeah, thanks a bunch, I feel like saying. We all know which friend.)

'Do you know what time she'll be back?'

'No, she didn't say.'

(Blimey, she sounds as cold as a polar bear's willie.)

'Could you tell her I called?'

'Yes, of course, goodbye.'

My God, talk about closing ranks. Lucy obviously really stuck the boot in as far as I was concerned. Her mum sounded as if I'd tortured her little girl to within an inch of her life. She is turning into Mrs Robinson.

I decide to take Rover out for a walk to take my mind off things (female things). Luckily Mum and Dad are still out so I don't have to talk as I go downstairs. When I get back, I hear the phone ringing. I dash inside and pick it up.

'Hello, is that Joe?' It's Lucy.

'Hi, Lucy, thanks for calling back. How you doing?'

'I'm fine, thanks. Mummy said you called earlier.'

'I just want to talk to you, if it's possible.'

'OK, but I'm not really sure what there is to say.'

'I just wanted to talk about what happened and stuff.'

'I'm sorry, Joe, but it's a little late. I'm seeing someone else, as you know.'

'Look,' I whisper, 'I can't talk on the phone, Mum and Dad are listening. (White lie no. 413B.) Can I meet you somewhere?'

'I'm ever so tired, couldn't we make it some other time.'

(I bet she's bloody tired. James Burton's enough to wear anyone out.)

'Are you on your own?'

'I am actually, Mummy and Daddy have gone out to supper with the Carter-Browns up the road.'

Christ, I think, she lives on a different planet to me. When was the last time my mummy and daddy went 'out to supper' with double-barrels?

'I could be over to your house in fifteen minutes. Please, Lucy, it's important. I really am missing you.'

'I'm sorry, Joe, of course you can come over, but not for too long, I want an early night. I'm going to Brighton tomorrow with . . . well, anyway, I'm going to Brighton.'

And we all know who bloody with! I *don't* say.

Pants and more pants.

Scene 25

Lucy's place.
Saturday 8.45 p.m.

ACTION:

Why is it whenever you split up with anyone, *they* instantly look ten times better and you feel ten times worse? When I arrive, all hot and sweaty from cycling, Lucy's looking more fab than ever, wearing white tracksuit bottoms, and the smallest, shortest T-shirt I've ever seen, designed to show off her gorge flat tummy and a couple of other major assets. A week or so ago I could have had my hands all over her right away but now there's a twenty metre fence between us (with about 3,000 volts zapping through it). We sit down at either end of the huge white sofa.

Lucy opens the batting.

'I don't know if this is such a good idea, Joe. I really haven't got a lot to say. I'm sorry about what happened but it wasn't working, not for me anyway.'

'I – er – just wanted to say sorry. I've been a bit of a jerk. I had a lot on my mind.'

'Well it was probably a bit my fault as well – I always go in a bit too heavy at the beginning.'

(Jeez, that wasn't too bad.)

'So, you forgive me sort of?'

'Sort of.'

'So that's all all right then.'

'Yeah, sure.'

This is a doddle – tee hee.

'So are we still going out?'

She looks at me as if I've just grown another head.

'Of course not. Sorry, Joe, I told you over a week ago.'

'But you said you'd forgiven me.'

'I have, but that doesn't mean I want to go out with you any more. You still won't know how to treat a girlfriend. Nothing will have changed there.'

'Ah, but that was then. I now know I can do it better. I've seen the shining light. Praise the Lord.'

Maybe a joke might lighten things up a bit. It obviously doesn't.

'Don't be silly, Joe, I'm being serious. The only shining light you've seen lately is in the mirror. You're far too into yourself to care about anyone else. You just want me on *your* terms – when it suits you. Lots of boys are like that. I'm quite lucky, I've been able to choose. Some girls can't.'

'But I . . .'

'You rang me because you were feeling a bit lonely, probably fancied a snog or something. (*Actually it was the snog AND 'something' I fancied.*) Sorry, Joe, I'm not that easy. That's why I said you should go for someone like Jade. She fancies one guy one minute and another the next.'

'So you don't fancy me any more.'

(Shit, this is now going terribly.)

She looks at me with a pained expression. 'Poor old Joe, you really don't get it, do you? It isn't down to whether I fancy you or not. Sure you look quite cute, but that's not nearly enough.'

'So James Burton *has* got enough, has he?'

'I'm sorry, but that's nothing to do with you.'

'Well has he?'

'OK, if you must know, James is probably the most grown-up boy I've ever been out with.'

'Why, just because he drives his dad's flash car?'

(You might have guessed – I can't drive and my dad's only got a twelve-year-old Mondeo.)

'That's nothing to do with it. He's kind and considerate and makes me feel special – sort of grown up. You and I were just like kids mucking about. Look, Joe, I'm really sorry, but I don't think there's much point in this. It never really worked with us and that's it. If we don't stop now, someone's going to say something really nasty.'

'Won't you give it another go, please.'

'You still don– . . .'

'Pleeeease. I'm on special offer this week.'

'Look, Joe, let's stop right now, before this gets silly. The one thing I really liked about you was that I thought you were cool. Not the sort of cool I wanted, as it turned out, but cool all the same. Don't blow that for God's sake by being a saddo. Now, watch my lips . . . I, Lucy Martin, no longer want to go out with you, Joseph Derby. No hard feelings, but that's the way it is.'

It's beginning to sink in that she really isn't joking.

She's still talking.

'Joe, I think you ought to go. Sorry if I've upset you, but I could have said all this over the phone. Look, I'm really tired and I want to go upstairs to my room.'

Bloody hell. A couple of weeks ago I could have gone upstairs with her.

I walk out to my bike and without turning round, cycle slowly down the road feeling mighty pissed off. Bloody cow! Upset me? Me? What a cheek. Who does she bloody think she is? I bet the only reason she prefers him is because of his dad's car. It's her that can't keep a relationship going. Christ, it didn't take long for her to find someone else. There'll probably be another along in a fortnight – like buses. I reckon I'm lucky to be out of it. Saved in the nick of time. She'd better not come back to me when it's all over. I won't have her in the house after this.

Mind you, she did look gorge.

When I get home I ring Merlin.

'Hi, Merlin, you'll never guess what's happened.'

'You've had a baby.'

'No stupid, this is serious. I've just done something really uncool. I just went back and sort of pleaded with Lucy to have another go.'

'What'd she say?'

'She made out I was too into myself to have a proper relationship.'

'Yeah, so what? Well done! You never get anywhere if you don't look after yourself first.'

'Yeah, but she's now going out with James Burton.'

'Flipping hell, I bet that makes you feel a right nerd.'

'Thanks a lot. It does, as it happens. She said he's kind and considerate.'

'Did she also mention the fact he's a top-class, fully paid up dickhead? I wouldn't even let my sisters go out with anyone like that, and that's saying something. You're better off out of it, mate.'

'Yeah, but I really miss her.'

'You've forgotten what I said the other day. Anyway, don't worry, she'll soon find out what that muppet Burton's all about. Just thank your lucky stars it's not me you're up against.'

Good old Merlin.

Scene 26

The Kingdom of Joe Derby.
Same night – later.

ACTION:

It's about two in the morning and I can't get Lucy off my mind. I keep thinking of her pretty face (and that T-shirt). How could she do it to me? And all for James bloody Burton. It's such a total balls-up! What was it she said? He's so kind and considerate and knows just how to treat a girl. I wonder just *how* well she lets him treat her? I wonder what they get up to?

And another thing. I bet she's already told him that I'm just a little boy and not worth bothering with. It's all too crap for words. I can just hear her, telling him, in that soft little voice of hers, how she's really into whatever he's into. He's captain of the school cricket team, so I suppose she'll have pictures of bloody cricketers and stumps and balls and everything all round her poxy room – with all the film posters thrown into the bin.

Oh yeah, and I bet her dad, John, slaps him on the back and calls him 'old man' and talks about the test match and all that sort of stuff, like those nerds at school who bring their stupid radios in to catch the stupid scores in the breaks. If there's one thing more boring than watching cricket, it has to be listening to it:

'There's trouble lurking at the pavilion end – the silly mid-

on's just got his *deep square leg caught up in his short slip.*'
Or something.

And if there's one thing more boring than listening to cricket, it's talking about it. So I won't.

Oh yeah and I can just see her mum looking him up and down, like she did me that afternoon. Burton's much straighter and more grown-up looking than I am, so he probably goes down even better (so to speak). The old *Graduate* fantasy rears its ugly head again.

Rover starts to snore and whenever that happens the only way to shut him up is to put my hand over his nose. I think he must have been dreaming, as he wakes up and stares round the room in sheer terror. I wonder what dogs dream about? Perhaps there's some canine equivalent to Jade who he's been trying to get off with down the park. Mind you, the last time I saw him try anything of an amorous nature, apart from someone's leg, was with a massive Rottweiler, who was not only too tall, but much, much worse – a bloke. I think it fair to report it didn't go down too well at all. Poor old Rover came scurrying back to me as fast as his little legs would carry him and I had to try to stop the bloody thing from tearing his head (or my arm) off. It was just like a scene from 'Tom and Jerry'.

So what do I do about Lucy? I suppose I'd better put her in the good old things-that-went-pear-shaped-due-to-me-being-a-prat box (if it's not full up). The most important thing, for all concerned, is that I get my cool back. I can't believe I actually almost begged her to give me another chance. She'll be sorry when I'm a famous film director. And then there's Jade.

Talking of Jade, didn't she ask me to go up to her room some time? She said she'd find me something nice as I remember. The trouble with her is, when I play it cool it works really well, but I know if I try to make the running it'll almost certainly go wonky. It's as if I can't do anything until she asks first. It's a drag, because it means I have to hang around looking sort of cool and detached in the hope that she'll notice and have another go. Then there's the old problem of what do I do if she wants to do the whole thing – like going the whole way. At least if I did go the whole way with Jade, she wouldn't be breaking the law now I'm sixteen. Although if I did it with Lucy, I would.

The way I feel at the moment, I wouldn't mind sharing a cell with either of them.

Scene 27

Northbridge High School.
One week later, 8.50 a.m.

ACTION:

Merlin comes into the schoolyard practically wetting himself with glee. He's just picked up the *Northbridge Gazette* on the way in and is dying to show it to everyone. He opens it on the centre spread and there we are, me and him, with the gorgeous Labardia sisters (and a load of stuffed pets in the background), looking like we'd just come from the Planet Cool. I don't believe it – me in the flipping papers.

'What does it say?' I ask, trying to read over Merlin's shoulder.

'Hang on, give us a chance, you haven't admired the picture long enough.'

By this time there's a small group of our mates grouped round us. Merlin starts by reading the headline:

Hollywood Comes to Northbridge

'Naff or what?' yells Spike. 'Things only ever go *from* Northbridge.'

Everyone tells him to shut up, and Merlin continues:

'Two future stars of the movie industry are beginning their careers at our very own Northbridge High School. Merlin Labardia and Joseph Derby, from Year Eleven, treated the rest of the school, on Thursday evening, to the world première of a film they have produced called La Maison Doom. *A riotous time was had by all as the macabre but hilarious story unfurled of two French girls, played by Jade and Sky Labardia, who set about wreaking revenge on their wicked father (played by their real father, Tony Labardia) and all mankind. What could so easily have slipped into an extremely nasty and perverted experience, was skilfully turned on its face into true farce in the time-honoured* Carry On *tradition.*

'I think we can all safely say "watch this space", as the two young film-makers are already planning to go on to bigger and better things.'

'Are we?' I ask Merlin when we're by ourselves.

'Well, I don't actually remember saying so, but I suppose we must be.'

'Like *what* bigger and better things?'

'Blimey, give us a break, I don't know. Perhaps we should do more comedy.'

'What do you mean?' I say sarcastically. 'We haven't done *any* yet – not on purpose anyway. Don't tell me you've already forgotten it was only funny by accident.'

'Well, I always knew it had comic potential,' replies Merlin cockily.

'You lying toad, you had no more idea than I had. You can fool all the others but not me.'

'OK, but it doesn't mean we can't do it again, does it? Who knows, now we know what we're doing we could make it even funnier.'

'Yeah, and it could fall flat on its flipping face.'

Just then Lucy comes by. I haven't seen or spoken to her since Saturday week, when I made such a prat of myself. Oh no, she's coming over. Don't say she's going to rub my nose in it in front of Merlin.

'Hi, Joe. What's it like to be a star? I just saw your picture in the local paper. You look fab.'

I glance across the yard and see several of her mates holding the *Northbridge Gazette* and giggling. Now how the heck do I handle this? She said she'd always thought I was cool, so just let's show her how bloody cool I can be.

'Oh that, yeah, the camera never lies, so I'm told.'

Merlin hides the paper, gives me a thumbs-up behind her back and strolls off.

'I haven't seen you since our chat. I wanted to know if you were all right.'

'Fine, thanks. Just had a lot on – what with the film and everything.'

Hey, I'm beginning to enjoy this.

'I'm afraid I didn't see it, I had to do something else that evening.'

Oh yeah, I bet you did, I think to myself, and I know who with.

'Everyone says it was brilliant,' she adds. 'You didn't tell me it was funny.'

'You didn't ask,' I reply rather smugly.

'I wondered if I could have a private viewing some time?' she asks.

Hang on! What game's she playing now?

'Won't Mr Burton mind? I thought you two did everything together these days.'

'Oh him, he's such a pompous jerk.'

'But you said . . .'

'You really mustn't believe everything a girl tells you, Joe.' Lucy smiles and gives me an innocent-little-girl pout.

At that moment the bell goes and she rushes off to her class, leaving me like a beached whale. Who does she bloody think she is?

I'm strolling to the school entrance when old Ma Dixon comes round the corner from the staff car park.

'Ah, Joseph . . .'

I whip round to see if she's talking to someone behind me. She's never ever called me Joseph before . . . a load of other things, but not Joseph.

'. . . I was reading the local paper this morning and saw that you're about to become a star. Well done, young man, I always knew you had it in you. Why I was only saying to Mrs Bridges in the common room –' Blah-blah-blah . . .

I won't even repeat what she says. It's hardly believable that only a couple of weeks ago she was willing to see me hung, drawn and bloody quartered by the boss for answering back.

'. . . I can only hope,' she droans on, 'that when you're

rich and famous, I might be able to claim to have played some small part in your success –' Blah-blah-blah.

I think everyone on the planet's gone mad today.

As for being famous, who knows what it would do to me. Probably send *me* bonkers. At least Merlin's fairly bonkers already, so it won't make much difference. Anyway, how could anyone ever be famous coming from a family like mine?

Fat chance!

Merlin's dungeon.
Monday 5.00 p.m.

ACTION:

Merlin and I have come back to his place to try and work out what we're going to do next, filmwise. Neither of us have ever tried to do comedy so it's not going to be easy.

'Let's just chuck every idea in the middle and see where we get to,' I suggest.

'I think it should be a sort of piss-take of something that's already been done,' Merlin replies, as he comes back with the teas. 'Like something quite serious, which we turn on its head.'

'How's about doing a movie about a soap like "Hollyoaks" and then turn it round?'

Merlin thinks for a bit. 'Did you see *The Killing of Sister George*? It was on telly the other week. It's the movie where Beryl Reid, who's the star of this soap, gets killed off. She was a district nurse, I think.'

'We could do it even better. We could get one of the main characters to go mad and shoot the writer – in real life. Yeah, he's been knocking off one of the other stars and when the writer finds out, he threatens to write him out of the soap because he fancies her too.'

'Have you got any better ideas?' Merlin asks.

'I've always wanted to do one of those wildlife

programmes like David Attenborough does, but make it all go wrong.'

Merlin looks puzzled. 'How do you mean?'

'Well, you know they always try to tell some naff story.'

'I don't even watch them, I think they're really boring.'

'Well, anyway,' I say. 'I reckon they make the whole thing up to make it more interesting.'

'How? I thought the whole point was that it was real.'

'OK, let's take an example. In one scene, we get little Willie the wombat at home with his mum, in a hole, or a tree or whatever they're supposed to live in. Next we get a scene where naughty little Willie strays away and is suddenly all alone in the outback – lost.

'Enter a dingo (or something) which prowls around hungrily. The bloke who's telling the story, cleverly makes a link, even though the two animals are never seen on the screen together. One second it's Dennis the dingo licking his lips, the next it's Willie the wombat looking dead scared. Then you either get Dennis the dingo, chewing on some unidentifiable lump of furry meat (supposed to be our Willie) or our Willie safely back with his mum, followed by a very pissed-off Dennis. You see – it's all made up from little bits of footage strung together to make the whole dreary business more interesting.'

'So you reckon you could take the footage and make

it anything you want,' Merlin asks, beginning to show interest.

'Yeah, you could have the baby wombat eating the dingo if you wanted.'

'It would be difficult to do. You'd have to get hold of all the film.'

'No, you could just pinch it off the telly.'

Merlin looks thoughtful. 'Actually, I've got another idea about animals. Do you remember that stupid programme, "One Man and His Dog"?'

'Is that the one where farmers used to compete to see whose dog round up the sheep best? Talk about pants,' I mutter.

'Yeah, it used to be on Sundays, just after God.'

'What about it? It doesn't sound very exciting.'

Merlin bursts out laughing. 'It would be if they did it with the sheep rounding up a whole load of dogs. Sort of "One Man and His Sheep".'

'Yeah, OK, but I can't see it making a whole film.'

'What if the farmer falls in love with the sheep? That would make a great secondary plot.'

'Too close to real life? Some farmers have very odd relationships with their sheep.'

'No, it's brilliant, it brings a bit of gritty reality into it. It'll appeal to perverts and animal lovers alike,' Merlin giggles.

'And country lovers.'

'And people who're into "Pet Rescue".'

'I'd hardly call it being rescued,' I add.

We both fall about laughing.

'D'you think we'd get away with it?' I ask almost seriously.

'I don't see why not,' says Merlin. 'If we make it funny enough.'

'Like we *didn't* mean to last time, you mean.'

'Look, we're just going to have to forget that. Hang on a minute, maybe we don't try to forget it. Maybe it was the fact that we tried to shoot it absolutely straight which was what everyone found funny.'

'So maybe we choose the most ludicrous plot and shoot it as if we don't see the joke.'

'Blimey, Joe, I think we've maybe cracked it. The only problem we had with *La Maison Doom* was *not* realising how daft the plot really was. There was nothing wrong with the way we did it at all.'

'There'd be a few practical problems,' I say.

'Like what? We can borrow a whole load of dogs from kids at school. It'll be funnier if they're all different. Then all we have to do is find a sheep.'

'Not just any old sheep, it'll have to be the cleverest sheep in the world.'

Merlin thinks for a bit.

'Why don't we dress a sheepdog up in a sheepskin.'

'Won't it get a bit hot?'

'Joe, are you mad, or just trying to be difficult? All right, clever-dick, we'll shave the blinking sheepdog and then shove it in the sheepskin.'

'So much for the cleverest sheep in the world.'

'I've got an even better idea. Remember when we ate the pork that was supposed to be Monsieur Leblanc.'

'Yeah,' I say nervously. There really are no limits to where Merlin's weird mind can go when it's on a roll.

'Well, when the farmer's wife spots the growing relationship between her husband and the prize-winning sheep, she gets real jealous and kills it and serves it up for Sunday lunch. Her old man then eats his new sort of girlfriend. End of story.'

'You had to get murder in somewhere, didn't you?'

'It's only a sheep. We've eaten hundreds of them, and they didn't exactly die in their sleep.'

'I suppose so, if you put it like that,' I admit rather sheepishly.

'Joey boy, I think we've just hit on the funniest plot in the world. Now all we've got to do is forget it's remotely out of the ordinary and try to shoot it like a documentary.'

Oh no, here we go again!

Scene 29

My house.
Monday 7.30 p.m.

ACTION:

I can't get over what Lucy said in the schoolyard. All that stuff about me being a kid and more into myself than anyone else, seems now to have gone out of the window. And now the wonderful, caring, considerate, knows-how-to-make-a-girl-feel-special James Burton, is just a pompous jerk. If I didn't know better, I'd think it was *her* that was playing games, and twisting us blokes round *her* little finger. What a nerve!

I'm just about to start thinking about my homework, when Mum, sounding all excited, calls from the bottom of the stairs.

'Joe, it's Lucy. I didn't think you were still friends.'

I stroll slowly down the stairs and count to ten seconds before picking up the phone.

'Hi, how you doing?'

'Hello, Joe, I'm glad you're still speaking to me.'

'Why not? I have to tear myself away from the mirror sometimes,' I reply, sounding all hurt.

'Look, I didn't really mean all that stuff. It was just something I said because you put me on the spot.'

'Hang on, Lucy, I didn't ask you to go out with James Burton. How do you think I felt being thrown over for a dickhead like him?'

'I didn't think you cared very much either way.'

'I had a lot on my mind, what with the film and my gran dying and everything.'

(Oh no, I've used the dead granny card after all, and she hadn't even died yet.)

'Does that mean you *do* still care about me?'

'Yeah! Of course.'

'Can we see each other again?'

Now for the performance.

'Well, I'm not sure, Lucy. You really hurt me. How will I ever be able to trust you? It takes me a long time to get over things like this.'

'Look, I'm really sorry – please say you will.'

'Well OK, I'll think about it. I'll see you at school. I've got to go now, I've got homework.'

I put the phone down and punch the air. Game, set and match. Just as I'm about to leap up the stairs, the phone goes again. Somehow I know it's for me.

'Hello, is that Joe?'

'Yeah, who's that?'

'It's Jade – remember me?' she giggles.

As if I wouldn't. Blimey, this is the first time she's ever phoned me.

'Hi, Jade, how you doing? Everything all right?'

'I wondered if you remembered that I said I'd show you something you might be interested in, in my room? I'm just looking at it now, and I wondered if you weren't doing anything, whether you'd like to come round and see for yourself.'

I remember her room full of mirrors and I can hardly speak.

'Er, yeah, I mean no – um – I'm not doing anything. I'd love to. I'll see you in ten.'

Look, don't blame me!

The End?